Past the Future

Nathaniel Robert Winters

BUFFALO PRINTINGCOMPANY
Napa Valley California

Copyright 2014   by Nathaniel Robert Winters

"Those who don't learn from history will find they repeat previous made mistakes. Those who learn from history will find they repeat previous made mistakes unless they go out and change it." David O'Brien

Past the Future

Chapter 1

2125

I'm so groggy but try to focus. I hear the following coming from an antenna attached to the back of my head:

Sony-Audi-Google (SAG) is proud to unveil the latest in baby technology for 2125. As everyone knows you must start a new baby with a great mother-board. Our 2125 model comes with our newly improved motherboard with 1,000,000 gigs of RAM with the latest stem cell developments. SAG's new "Jordish" model comes with a non-sexual uni-body guaranteed to last 200 years or 1,000,000 miles, whichever comes first.

All race's genetic codes are included, and the new model comes in 50 glorious colors The new motherboard put last year's brain-core to shame with twice the speed.

So, when you are ready to complete your family, think of Sony-Audi-Google. Remember: "When you are ready, SAG is ready for you."

This advertisement is the first thing I hear as I come out of my induced coma. I am a twenty-first century man waking up in the twenty-second century.

The United States, which by 2052 included Canada and Mexico, returned to manned space flight after The United Arab States started a space program. There's nothing like a new cold war to induce space innovation. The Arabs with all their oil money decided to explore space and wanted to land on one of Saturn's or Jupiter's moons to look for natural resources. Most commodities on Earth were getting scarce.

The last thing I can remember—before my old-school attached antenna picked up this baby ad—I was rocketing on an experimental flight to Titan, Saturn's biggest moon. My robot companion, Mercury, named after the first US manned space ships, warned: "Dave, something is seriously wrong with the spaceship. Fuel has been leaking. I am going to implement emergency alternative *Van Winkle*."

"Are you sure, Mercury? That's a pretty radical program," I said.

It would mean all other options for safe return to Earth were not available. It would put me into an induced coma, inside a life-support bubble. The ship's other programs would be shut down and I would drift into space until NASA Control could find some way to rescue me.

This alternative was experimental. While *Van Winkle* had been built into all of this model of spacecraft, it had never been used. It was the last resort for a desperate situation.

"Yes, Dave that is the only way to save you. I am sorry. Good luck Dave. You will be asleep in 10, 9, 8, 7, 6, 5, 4, 3, 2…"

Chapter 2

A New Brave New World?

Consciousness comes to me slowly in this new century. The advertisement unnerves me as I struggle to awaken. Hospital buzzers sound and a team of workers come running to my aid.

Welcome to 2125," the strange looking man said with what I think is a smile. "I am Jordish-Michael number 7062, your lead doctor. You are a lucky man. We found your spacecraft drifting outside the solar system. We pulled your craft back to earth.

"An examination showed that your central nervous system was still alive. Our stem cell technology replaced all your damaged body systems."

The new style man talking to me had a humongous head. His skin was bright green. Each of his hands had seven fingers, including three dexterous thumbs.

"Thank you," was all I could manage to say, totally unnerved and shocked realizing I had been drifting in space for 73 years.

* * *

I learn quickly about 22nd century society. War and disease are a thing of the past. The new models of humanity have been genetically programed to get along. They are amazingly intelligent. Mental illness was defeated by genetic engineering.

With all these advancements, I feel something is missing. The architecture, dance and music of this culture are beautiful but lacking in something. What is it? I struggle to figure it out.

After many 22nd century novels are beamed to my cerebrum, I realize what is missing.

Without the crazy genotype, the new society has lost the rebels. These modern "humans" are genetically programed to get along, go with the flow. True innovation is sacrificed. Radical change in style is stifled. There are no Kurt Vonnegut, Stephen King, H. G. Wells or Susan B. Anthony types of people in this environment. Without mutation and natural selection I figure humanity is stuck on a nondescript treadmill.

Unfortunately, I now have other more immediate and personal things to worry about. I have to somehow get out of this God forsaken hospital. But I'm trapped. My new bones are not yet hardened enough to walk.

Jordish-Michael number 7062 is planning to do surgery on me tomorrow; modernizing me. I will be getting a new antenna implanted. Also I will have my "unnecessary" sex organ removed.

Chapter 3

Reprieve

I awoke in darkness assuming it was the middle of the night. I'm not surprised, after my induced sleep for so many years. I wondered how long it would take me to get a normal sleep cycle in this abnormal 22nd century.

Etes barely opened, I noticed two surgically dressed hospital personnel grabbing my gurney.

I protested, "It's not daylight, you're not moving me to surgery are you?"

"Quiet," the man said through his surgical mask. "You don't want to wake the staff and lose anything of importance, do you?" He placed a finger on his mouth signaling me to hush.

He had me convinced to keep my mouth shut.. It hit my brain; the man when he signaled had only five fingers.

The two pulled me off the bed into an exoskeleton framework. With a joystick one of them controlled my movements.

"Why do I suddenly feel like an insect?" Noticing my body moving from the outside in, with someone else controlling my movements, I felt like an ant on a leash.

We boarded a vehicle of some type and I felt it glide. The interior was leathery, gigantic, without windows. I could not tell our speed or where we were going. Despite it's size the vehicle was mostly empty.

One of the two men who moved me sat down next to my encased exo-body thing and said, "You probably have questions. I can answer some simple things; more will be revealed to you in a short period of time."

"Great, another mystery. I'm not confused enough yet?"

"Well Dave, I can tell you, you're safe. My name is Roger and I'm part of a group called The Renegades. We are not outlaws but we're on the outside of society because we refused to go along with modern norms.

"You might have noticed that we appear to have our original body parts. That is correct, including the parts under our clothing."

"How come they didn't give me that choice?"

"Probably because you are now so well known, it wouldn't be good for business."

"Business, really."

Roger smiled a knowing smile. "Yes Dave, the world is now run by corporations, not countries. Countries devolved as corporations got bigger and people kept moving."

"Why the change?"

People were moving all over the world. Nations became irrelevent as employees looked to companys to set rules and patterns.

"Wow, that's a lot to take in, but it also explains the advertising beamed right into my head. What type of transport is this? There aren't any windows."

"It's called a Jonah. Most of the world is underwater, so this is what your time would have called an ultimate green submarine. We are in the belly of a genetically altered whale. This Jonah is in a symbiotic relationship with man. We feed the Jonahs harvested blue-green algae. They transport us. One whale holds up to 350 seated passengers."

I tried to process it all , but just shook my head. "What corporation invented this?"

"I see you're catching on. Something called Grant Eckford."

"What percentage of people are Renegades?"

"A generation ago it was about 15 percent. Now it's down to about 10."

"My parents were Renegades, had me the old fashioned way. But the pressure to change is great. You can't get a good professional job when you are a Renegade. They don't think we are smart enough and they don't give maternity leave."

"So, what do you do for work?

"Mostly menial jobs on small farms and bartering. I think I should add that there is no evidence the big head brains make them smarter but now that skin color no longer is a racism factor we are scapegoated."

"Remember they are not smarter then you."

"Thanks, that's good to know and Roger, I'm very thankful you saved the family jewels, Yet, I can't help but wonder, what's in it for you and the Renegades? I wasn't born yesterday. Actually, more like a century ago. What do you want?"

"You're quite perceptive Mr. O'Brien. It will all be revealed in the lunch meeting."

"Ah, lunch. It's nice to know people still eat the same way."

Roger frowned and gave me a funny look. "What?"

"Growers Medtech Inc. is developing food hookups. In five years, most people won't need to eat."

"God, no food, no sex, what will they do for fun."

"Well, there are always the Instagram booths."

I didn't even ask.

He said. "Virtual reality, refreshing canned fun in just 30 seconds."

"Lord help me."

"They don't do that either, pray in public. Standardized religion is beamed directly into the brain for one minute a day. There is only one religion now."

"Of-course there is. Which one won?"

"It's multi-interchangeable, taking the best from all of them."

"Really? How did they decide that?"

"By corporate committee, of course."

"Of course," I repeated, laughing at the nonsense of it all.

"It's almost time for the lunch meeting. Do you want to ask me anything else, quickly?"

We had changed vehicles to a large truck-like ambulance. We were now back on land. There is a window. I see Irish green hills and turquoise blue water.

"Yeah, Roger. Where on earth are we?"

"The Berkeley Hills, in what used to be California, USA. That's where most of the Renegades live."

"Finally, something that makes sense. Where else would the non-normals live?"

Chapter 4

Business Lunch

There were ten in the room, including Roger and me. Six were Renegade types, four were modern. I was introduced to all by Roger. I suddenly realized he was much more important than he had let on.

Before anyone spoke, a group of legal documents were presented for me to sign by men I assumed were modern-type lawyers, their seven digits surrounding the tablet.

They weren't only getting my signature but also took a brain-scan of my sincerity. (How much could society get done if you couldn't lie a little on your paperwork? Paperwork, still called that even though paper hadn't been used for over a hundred years.) They had me swear to keep all information disseminated secret.

Who in this world would I tell anyway? Roger, reading my brain-scan, explained that I might meet some people in the future I might want to share information with. I thought--creepy, loudly, so he could hear it. That's creepy, Roger. Get out of my head. I shrugged in surrender and signed.

Lisa and Frank were Mods from the FBI (Federated Business Incorporated). They did for the Corporate Board of Directors (similar to the old US Senate) what the old FBI did for the dissolved US Government. They find out what's going on—when something's going on.

Benjamin and Anthony were the VIPs of the group, like senators, they were Directors of the Corporate Board.

Two normal human types, the last two, introduced to me as Annie Oakley and Sitting Bull.

"The real Annie Oakley and Sitting Bull? Is this all some kind of joke?"

"No joke. It's Sitting Bull and Annie Oakley from the 19th century," Benjamin said.

"Well I'll be a monkey's uncle."

Benjamin, the board member, said, "You know that evolution would tell us the monkey would actually be your uncle." Then he gave a chuckle.

I couldn't help myself his joke was so bad.

"Holy crap, is that what goes for humor with you types? Not many comedians, huh?"

"Actually, we have many comics, just a different type of humor from you Renegades." Benjamin responded.

"I've noticed. I guess losing sexual organs probably takes a lot of the fun out of funny," I said. The natural humans laughed, while the mods just sat straight faced. "Tough room."

Sitting Bull said, "Yeah. They're about as funny as a cavalry charge."

Annie cracked up. She slapped Sitting Bull's back. "Good one, Bull."

I said looking back to Benjamin, "Don't tell me. You have a time machine, don't you."

"It would appear you have figured out the obvious, Mr. O'Brien. What you don't know is that time machines have been made illegal. To much chance of undoing history.

"The first time machine was invented 24 years ago, in 2101. In early experiments, there was a danger that the time journeyers would interact with people in history. Such interaction could cause changes in the flow of history. Researchers thought this could be dangerous, so the Board of Directors discontinued all experimentation in 2115.

"We are making an exception in this case, Miss Annie Oakley and Mr. Sitting Bull are clones. The originals are back where they belong. Stem cells and cloning have come a long way while you were spaced out," he said.

"Miss Oakley and Mr. Bull were cloned as adults. They have all the memories of their lives before the cell transfers.

"Annie's clone is equal to the original at 25. She had an independent life and was cloned before becoming the star of Buffalo Bill's Wild West Show. Sitting Bull, age 30, had returned from Canada and was taken prisoner by the army. They sent the victor of Little Bighorn to Florida, away from his sacred land."

"What is even more important to our society—they both carry all their biological history. Annie and Bull have both been implanted with a computer chip, catching them up on the events and knowledge of this century."

"Why is their previous biological background so important?" I asked.

Benjamin smiled a very unnatural smile.

"That is why the three of you are here. We have a major problem developing quite quickly—a smallpox epidemic, mostly still confined to Asia, but it will probably spread."

"I thought you clone babies were disease proof."

"We are—or were, until this super virus strain showed up. But it's not natural. It came from a mix of a nineteenth century strain and a super strain developed by the old United States Government during the Cold War. Our research shows that only people vaccinated with the live virus are immune."

"Sitting Bull and Annie were both inoculated that way. Later in the 20th century, a weakened virus was used. You, as an astronaut, were immunized for almost everything with super inoculations. So, you are probably immune as well."

"How did the super strain get here from the Cold War period?" I asked.

A renegade by the name of Joe Smith illegally went back in time, gathered a sample of each virus and combined them. Then he came back here in 2125 and released the new strain.

"Joe Smith's distant ancestors were Mormons. We have captured him; he told us what he did. He was not happy with the current state of society in general, but especially, religion. He has some strong feelings about that and released the strain. Pandora is out of the box.

"He told us that he acquired the samples, from 1890, and during the Cold War, in 1963. We want you, Miss Oakley and Mr. Bull, to work as a team and go back in time to stop Mr. Smith before he takes the original virus from 1890 and builds that extra super smallpox strain and kills us all."

"You believe that is possible?" I asked.
"Not only possible but necessary."
"Why me?"

"Why you, indeed. Miss Oakley and Sitting Bull were picked for certain skills. You just happened along. But we believe that your knowledge of history and your astronaut training should make you quite useful."

"Why in the world would I volunteer?"

"Three reasons. Number one, compensation. Number two, to save humanity. And number three, how did you phrase it? To save your precious, *family jewels.*"

Chapter 5

Training

Bam! We were thrown together. The cowgirl, the Indian chief and an astronaut. We'd be the perfect opening line for a joke if I added ... "walked into a bar." Was I the only one who didn't see a fit in us becoming a winning team of time travel detectives? At least I had a PhD in history. But I'd missed weeks of training, and these futuristic Mods, or non-people, dropped me into this mess, literally from outer space.

I tried hard to play catch-up in the two weeks they gave me until our mission was to start. In many ways, I felt like I was back in astronaut training. Teammates doing hard physical and mental work to go off to . . . not space but the other side of Einstein's relativity reality . . . time.

***

After a full combat training we went out for what the Mods called pizza. Even though I hadn't had pizza in a century. This stuff tasted like cardboard, it wasn't even close to good. I sat across from my cohorts in a booth. The window afforded us a great view of the Pacific Ocean. San Francisco Bay had been engulfed by the rising ocean, due to climate change. What was left of the City of San Francisco were just the hills, sticking up as islands in the ocean, connected by boat traffic. I looked up to what used to be Nob Hill, now, Nob Island. A modern new Fairmont Hotel looked down from its perch at the top.

I started the conversation. "Bull, (that's what everybody called him) I've studied that Battle of Little Bighorn extensively. Most historians blame the US Army's loss on Custer's ego and ineptitude".

"I don't agree. Many great generals had big ego's—MacArthur and Patton from World War II come to mind. Further, Custer had a great track record in command during the Civil War. So I think it comes down to you and Crazy Horse."

"How were you going to overcome the US Cavalry's tremendous weapons superiority in an open field battle? They had both handguns and repeating rifles. Most of your men had just bows and arrows.

"Your advantage was numbers; you had a much bigger force. But that was only an advantage if you used it. You did, didn't you? You ordered all in. Everyone attacked at full stride on horseback, so the larger force could overwhelm the better equipped foe. Am I right?"

"Yes." He smiled which he didn't do often. I thought he might elaborate but he kept any details close to the vest like a football coach that might need to call the same play in a future game.

Finally, almost to cover the silence, he added, "We call it the Greasy Grass, not your Little Bighorn."

"Whatever name we use, I'm impressed by your tactics," I said.

"Because you didn't think an Indian could outsmart a white man?"

"Oh please, that way of thinking was over before I was born. I'm not in the least prejudicial. Great generals in history come from many races."

"How 'bout a girl. Can she outthink you?" Annie challenged.

"In your case, Annie, I know you can outshoot me. As for the thinking, let's hope both of us can outthink our foe when we go back in time."

"Amen to that," she said.

* * *

I took all my spare time exploring the evidence of our case. I learned that the time of departure and return on the time machine had to be set, before the subject or subjects left. Anybody who used it automatically left a DNA signature recorded on the time machine. It recorded where the subject went and from where they returned. Nothing else was known about their trip. The return time was set on the machine just before the device threw the package of DNA back in time. The machine was indifferent as to whether the molecules were of one person or of many.

Annie came over to me in the back of the study room. "What you doin', Spaceman?" (That had become Annie's nickname for me.)

"Just going over stuff you learned before I arrived. The time machine info."

"Want some help?" she asked.

I realized that I had been here almost a week and this was the first time Annie and I were alone.

I looked up from my notes and laughed. Annie had walked into the room almost silently. She was juggling five balls.

"What the heck are you doing?" I asked.

"Jugglin'."

"I know, why?"

"Helps my concentration. Shootin' at a moving target from a moving horse takes concentration. Jugglin' is like practice without practicin'."

"That makes sense. I like it."

A lot about this girl I liked. Women in the 1800s weren't supposed to be independent and confident. But she was different. Maybe it was her frontier spirit. I knew she was a winner.

She was also real smart, not knowledge smart; reasoning smart. Puzzles didn't puzzle her. And she was pretty, not like Hollywood gorgeous, but girl next door lovely and that red hair with those green eyes … I noticed my attraction. It had been a long long time since I had been next to a woman.

"You did fine in hand-to-hand combat today. You feel like your bones are all healed?" she asked.

"Yeah, I feel pretty good."

"Come on Spaceman, let's go get somethin' to eat. Then we can find a room and practice some one-on-one hand-to-hand . . . combat."

She giggled, "Why you lookin' at me like that? I've been away from home a long time too. I know how you've been sneakin' looks at me. A girl's got some needs too."

You see what I mean? A nineteenth century girl is just not supposed to be that forward.

I smiled and started to hear that song in my head, you know, the one from the Broadway musical about her? *Anything you can do, I can do better.*

Boy I hope so.

Chapter 6

It's a Riot

I arrived the next morning at the training center, well after Annie. We'd decided to be discrete. We didn't want our rendezvous to change any plans. He didn't say anything but I could tell Sitting Bull could sense a difference in us. I wondered if the secret could last another week, when my attention blasted in another direction.

A riot started in Berkeley with a group of Renegades attacking local Corporate Board headquarters. The smallpox epidemic had exploded, leaping swiftly across Europe. Rumors spread that the Corporation was purposefully disseminating the virus.

Why riots? Because the Renegades believed the Corporations were close to selling a cure, and wanted to maximize profits.

We could hear bullhorns outside, warning people to move back. Glass windows were crashing and shattering just outside our training center. Tear gas started trickling into the building, burning our eyes.

Benjamin from the Corporate Board moved to the front of the room. "These Renegade riots and paranoid rumors have forced a change in schedule. You must begin your mission today.

"Dave, you probably think you're not ready. But work as a team. Somehow, I believe you three will stop Joe Smith. Use any means necessary. Is that clear enough?

"Board the bus outside. It will take you to the time machine. Good luck and good hunting. The whole world is counting on you."

Chapter 7

Time Warp

The three of us, the Indian chief, the cowgirl and the spaceman, walked not into the bar of a bad joke but something stranger; a time machine; testing a theory of relativity that I could never fully understand. Why not, I thought, I couldn't build rockets either.

The machine's recorder keeps track of the travelers' entry points in time and space. Joe Smith went to Utah in September of 1890, six years before it became a state. Then just two weeks later, he was recorded being sent to 1963 Washington D.C.

We strapped down to the seats much like I would for a takeoff. Instead of rockets blasting, a ray engulfed the room. My head felt like it was splitting into pieces and pain shot throughout my body for a few seconds.

Suddenly, the machine stopped and sunlight slapped me in the face. We'd been sent to Utah just a half hour after Smith, re-materializing near the town of Ogden.

Ogden looked like one of those western towns in the movies. People walked along wooden sidewalks and horses and buggies filled the dirt streets. Dust loomed everywhere. One thing conveniently left out of those movies was the amount of horse manure everywhere; unavoidable. I must have stepped in it three times just crossing the street (yeccchhh).

We were outside of town, standing in the middle of a dirt road. I felt fine and Bull and Annie said they were "A-OK." (They stole that term after reading about the first space flights, as in, "Houston we are A-OK.")

After exploring the town we didn't spot Joe. Showing an antiqued picture, we asked everyone we encountered if they had seen him. I found a young women with a baby waiting for her husband. She'd seen our man buying a ticket to Salt Lake City.

"Seems like he knew someone would be coming after him and he wanted a head start," I said. The next train south was in 12 hours.

"It looks like we need horses," Bull said.

I hated that idea. I was a comparative novice with horses, while my teammates grew up on horseback.

"Don't worry, Spaceman, I got you covered for now." She bought me a small buckboard.

"Be careful," she teased, "you might get splinters."

Bull and Annie took off, leaving me in the dust. I followed, feeling quite inadequate.

Even in 1890, a train moved much faster than a horse. Our only chance was to find Smith in Salt Lake City or someone who saw him switch trains. Glancing at the newspaper purchased in Ogden, I found a different solution to finding our man:

April 5, 1890. A smallpox outbreak has taken off among immigrants in San Francisco's Chinatown. A special shipment of vaccine is being sent from a Chicago lab.

After digesting this information, Annie boarded our horses in Salt Lake while Bull and I beelined to the station and purchased tickets to San Francisco. It was the first train of the day, so Smith couldn't have beat us. We made it on with just minutes to spare.

I felt we had the advantage over Smith. We knew what he looked like, and he wasn't even sure anyone was after him. Yet after each of us checked extensively in all the compartments, we couldn't find Joe Smith.

After a calm but concerned discussion, I volunteered to go back to Salt Lake City and ask around while they continued on. Maybe he took a different route.

***

Back in the territory's capital, I started from scratch. Showing his picture, I asked if anyone knew his whereabouts. An hour after I started my quest, a man stumbled out of one of the few bars in town.

Mormons didn't drink but this guy either didn't get the message or was not part of the home-based religion. The soused gentleman told me Mr. Smith was in a small town named Smithville, just a few miles south.

I braved riding my horse to the town in question. True enough, Joe was making a speech to an audience that seemed hostile. After he told them he was a prophet, the town's leaders told Smith in no uncertain terms to get out of town immediately.

When he continued with the speech anyway, defying the town leaders, they lost their patience. Rifles appeared and a warning shot was fired. Smith finally gave it up and trotted his horse back to Salt Lake City.

I walked over to one of the men with a gun and asked, "What was that all about?"

He gave me an unfriendly look and asked, "Who are you?"

I offered my hand and said I was just passing through and was curious as to what was going on.

He said, "We are a private family and do not need no strangers snooping about. Now the Salt Lake City Leadership has applied to become a state and people have been real nosey. You can follow that crazy feller out of here and we won't have to shoot ya."

"Can I just ask you what he wanted and then I'll leave?"

"He claimed he was kin and was a prophet from the future. He ain't my kin and we don't need no crazy people attractin' no attention."

***

I remember reading that not all the Mormons wanted to go along with the leadership and give up multiple wives. I figured this was one of those groups. I left them to do whatever they wanted and followed Joe Smith back towards Salt Lake City.

I tried to stay well behind him but since we were both novice horseman, neither of us could set a consistent pace. The space between us dwindled until he knew I was riding behind. Not wanting him to think I was spying, I waved a hello. Joe waited for me to catch up. It appeared that I was going to get a first hand look at our nemesis.

We introduced ourselves and I had to ask, "Joe Smith, are you related to the Mormon founder?"

"Indeed, I can trace my lineage to that great man. Are you one of the faithful?"

"No, not me, my father came to America from Ireland just before my birth. I'm Catholic."

"So, what brings you to Utah?"

You, you crazy SOB, I thought, but said, "I was sent by a New York bank to see if we could do business here when statehood arrives."

"What do you think about that?" Joe asked.

"I was thinking it might be difficult because Mormons don't trust outsiders too much. What do you think, Mr. Smith?"

"I think you're probably right. If I were you I'd head back to town. Then I'd hightail it back to New York. Leave us Mormons to our own."

"What do you do, Mr. Smith?"

"Why Mr. O'Brien, I'm a banker."

We both had a good laugh. Never underestimate a guy with a good sense of humor.

I realized I could probably just take him out now. But I was not trained to be an assassin, not a cold-blooded killer. I wondered what Sitting Bull would do in my place. He killed many in war, but here and now, I didn't think he would pull the trigger. I wasn't sure about Annie. She was full of surprises.

As we rode into town I asked casually where he was going.

His eyes changed; I could almost see a kind of paranoia creeping into his mind.

After a gap, he said, "To visit family, good luck Mr. O'Brien." Then he trotted off.

If I followed I would give myself away. I went and sent a telegram to Bull and Annie.

Subject in Salt Lake stop

Not sure next move stop

Met him couldn't avoid stop

Smart, dangerous stop

Bet he goes SF today stop

Meet in Oakland stop

Salt Lake City was booming in growth and importance in 1890, doubling in population in the proceeding decade to over 40,000, a large metropolis in the western part of the country for the time. Utah was applying for statehood which was only six years away. Polygamy had just been banned. With Joe Smith's religious fervor and his knowledge of the future he could create some chaos here. But we knew he had to get the smallpox live virus sample and leave for the 1960s in ten more days.

***

I felt compelled to visit the almost completed Mormon Temple at the center of the city. That view, more than anything else so far, made me feel I was truly back in an historic era.

Compelled to get back to my reason for being here, I checked into the hotel across from the train station and watched for Smith. He didn't disappoint. Within an hour he walked in with a large group of men. My schedule showed a train going west in ten minutes. I planned to catch the next in two hours. Something was amiss. I wished our want-to-be Mormon boarded with less men.

Chapter 8

North by Northwest

Annie met me at the train station in Oakland. She yelled "darlin,'" and ran over and gave me a big kiss, then laughed at my embarrassment. Don't worry Spaceman, nobody knows us here and now.

Realizing she was right and Bull was off following Smith and gang, I said, "You think Bull can do without us for a hour? There is a hotel next to the station."

"Why Mr. O'Brien," said Annie, "if an hour's all you need we might as well be on our way." She giggled, took my hand, and led me across the street and into the lobby. Annie was just full of surprises.

We decided we might as well get a good night's sleep and saddle up first thing in the morning. Doing dinner, watching the sunset over the bay and out the Golden Gate before the bridge and long before most of San Francisco was underwater, was a thing of beauty.

"The red in that sunset is almost as pretty as your hair," I waxed poetic, hoping to impress the girl.

"Dave," she said, "don't get all mushy on me. Why don't we let nature do the talkin'."

"Point taken, Miss Oakley. See if I ever try to be romantic again."

"Dave, shut up and kiss me."

Yes, the girl was full of surprises, I could get used to this.

* * *

Settled and refreshed at sunrise, we went north, following a road along the east side of the bay. Bull was going to leave a special sign if they turned another way. One no one else would understand; a simple drawing of a rocket, nose pointing his direction. At the north side of the bay we saw the rocket and turned west. "I don't understand," I said. "Why doesn't he head for San Francisco to get the vaccine?"

Annie shrugged, "Makes no sense to me neither."

We ferried over Suisun Bay and the Napa River, south of the town of Napa, heading west over hills filled with amazingly tall redwood trees. The beauty was breathtaking but I knew not to mention that to Annie. She wouldn't want to hear any mushy stuff.

Then we saw Bull's rocket sending us northwest, away from the town of Santa Rosa, more towards the coast. After a day's full ride, we decided to make camp, still miles from the coast but well south of the Russian River.

* * *

The sun poured over the eastern hills as thick as maple syrup. Riding a horse all day left my legs feeling like pancake batter. Breakfast was beef jerky. Well, it was better than the liquid meals I often had to eat in space.

Annie rising out of our bedroll dressed in, well, in her undergarments, sun shining through her rose red hair made me want to quote poetry but I knew better. I just smiled at her.

"Put the puppy dog eyes away, Spaceman. We don't have no more time for that," she kissed the air in my direction. Annie had dressed and her horse was saddled before I could get to the cinch straps.

"Don't say anything. I wasn't born in this century. The only thing I did with horses was bet on them at a racetrack."

"Hope you didn't bet much, because what you know about them, my oh my. Not much."

"Well, can you drive a car?"

"You mean those things in the 21st century with power brakes and steerin'," she giggled and said, "try driving a stagecoach down a hill like they got in San Francisco, then we'll talk."

I think I just got "*anything you can do 'ed*" by the women they wrote the song about. Glad she's on my side.

Chapter 9

The Great Escape

By riding hard northwest for two hours, redwoods almost blocking the sun, we came to a crossroads. One road turned more to the north and I could see a small town ahead. The other ran east and west but no rocket was in sight. Suddenly, out of nowhere, Bull appeared. He signaled for us to be quiet and to follow him.

He took us west, where from a hill we could view most of the small town of Lone Pine. Bull had been scouting. He reported that there were two businesses in town, a market/post office and a roadhouse/bar. Add a few houses and about ten farms and that was it, population guess; 50, about 2-1 male.

Bull had tracked Joe Smith's group which now counted thirteen. Two women and one man had joined them in Oakland before the smallpox vaccine arrived from Chicago, so Smith still didn't have the vaccine. Why was he up here, in the middle of nowhere?

"I think the new three are married Mormon style."

"I guess all we can do is watch," I said.

"One thing I didn't tell you, Dave. They have three Gatling guns."

I tried to digest that fact. "Someone's expecting trouble. But they don't have the smallpox vaccine and time is getting short. He is due to time warp to the sixties in just four days. What the hell is he up to?"

Annie said, "I think it's time I found out."
She took off her cowgirl hat, gave it to me, smiled
and winked. Then, just like she did with the
pistols she carried, Annie took a shot. Fast as a
bullet, before I could stop her. She ran into the
Pine Grove store, came back out, fixed her hair,
and walked right into Smith's camp. I would find
out the details of that encounter later.

Smith personally greeted her. She told him
she was a local girl from a little town, west
towards the ocean. She said, I just had to find out
about the new men campin' out here."

"Are you single Miss?" Joe asked.

"Yes, I'm Ann Adams. Nice to meet ya'.

She did her best at flirting with Joe and the
other men. Let me tell you, she can be
captivating."

She almost danced among the men. "What are all you men doing in these parts?"

"Well Miss Adams we are looking for wives."

"All of you and just little ole' me. I feel like the Belle at the ball."

Smith said. "It stuffy in here, Miss Adams, care to take a walk?"

"Well as nice as that offer sounds I kinda' like the odds in here." She sashayed over to a young strong looking guy named Steve.

Joe Smith decided to take control. "I am the Bishop of this group and I will pick you a husband."

"Well maybe I'll be leavin' now."

"I'm afraid that's not possible. I'll be taking your gun. You will be our guest tonight. Don't worry, we'll keep you safe and sound. You won't be alone long. We will raid the town tomorrow and keep the women."

"What about the men?"

"I was hoping they would stay out of the way so we wouldn't have to kill them."

"Why in the world would you do that? What do you want?"

"The Mormon leadership in Utah are selling out. I know where that leads. We are going to start New Zion here. We need the women to be fruitful and multiply. You will stay tonight with Mr. Reese and Mr. Younger. Please don't try to get away. You're lovely and I wouldn't like you to get hurt."

Mr. Smith didn't know he was messing with the wrong girl. When he awoke the next morning, Reece and Younger were out cold and Annie was back safely with us.

Miss Oakley waited for Younger to fall asleep then smiled sweetly at Reece. "Come here," she said, taunting the big man. She grabbed his shirt, pulling him closer. Her lips kissed invitingly. He lay his rifle by the bed to probe for her body with his hand. Quick as a blink, **Swish**! The gun was in Annie's control, pointed at Reece's belly. **Shock**! He reached for her. **Blam**! He never saw the rifle butt hit his head.

The big man fell, awakening Younger. The second man came at her like a bear. **Pow**! The point of the rifle stabbed his solar plexus. He gasped for a breath before being clubbed by the butt, **Boom!** She turned his world black.

Annie pulled up the tent bottom, looked both ways and **Presto!** She disappeared from Smith's imagined harem.

After she escaped in the middle of the night, Annie alerted us to Smith's plan. We realized we had to evacuate Lone Pine as quickly and quietly as possible. We had to improvise a countermeasure at once. I thought of doing the Paul Revere thing but what would I yell? "Crazy Mormons from the future are coming." I don't think so.

It was time for some futuristic magic. I had been collecting some minerals during our travels that I thought might have some use, mostly prosperous and sulphur. I lit fire to an old empty barn just to the south of Lone Pine. I added the chemicals and it glowed like the sun was coming up.

Annie and I knocked on each door yelling, "**Fire**." Nothing makes people scamper faster than a fire. Everybody scurried to the unusually glowing barn.

I had their attention now and they had all seen the Mormon group that camped just outside of town in tents. They heard them practicing shooting. But that would be normal behavior for a hunting party. How do I convince the townspeople that the group is dangerous?

Annie had given me permission to tell them she was the famous Annie Oakley.

Many had seen her image on billboards. A young man had seen the show in San Francisco. He shouted, "By gosh it's actually Annie Oakley!"

Annie said, "My friend, Dave here is telling you the truth. The men in the tents are dangerous and have Gatling guns. We need to retreat. Get your weapons and follow him."

By dawn when Joe Smith found out that Annie was gone, the townspeople were up on an observation hill behind a rock outcropping.

Chapter 10

Clone

"We have more people, they have the firepower," Sitting Bull said, and laughed.

I threw a chuckle, "It's not the same as Little Bighorn."

"No, it's not," he agreed. If we all rushed them we'd be torn to shreds by those guns.

"It reminds me of World War I, when machine guns dominated and defenses destroyed the attackers until near the end with the development of the tank," I said.

Bull said, "We don't have any tanks so I suggest we play defense. Those three Gatling gun are not very mobile."

"I agree. Let's get the people to dig a trench," I suggested to Bull and Annie.

"You realize he still doesn't have the vaccine."

Annie said, "None of this makes sense. Why would he come up here and do all this if he is leaving in two days."

"I took a long look at Annie Oakley. My Annie Oakley, and now Lone Pines'. But she wasn't the real Annie Oakley and the man next to me was not the real Sitting Bull. It hit me like a heavyweight boxer's punch before they banned the sport in 2043.

I said to my two friends, "The Joe Smith they captured in 2125 was *also* not the real Joe Smith, but a clone. Think about it, the super virus from the 1960s would have the DNA of this era as well as any before 1960. The Mods must have known that.

"So why send us back here?" Annie asked.

"To stop this guy from recreating history. Later, he might get the virus and wreak total havoc."

Bull said, "I didn't like the society of the Mods in 2125 and I like them less now."

Annie and I nodded in agreement.

Chapter 11

Smith's Sebastopol

Smith's group attacked the town. They took over the buildings but realized they had lost the element of surprise. They captured no one. The women were safe behind rocks on the hill.

Turning the Gatling guns around they pounded the hill and under a hail of bullets they tried a frontal assault. Annie had borrowed a Sharps buffalo gun from a townie and out of range from the Gatling fire she picked off two of Smith's soldiers, hitting each in the leg, reluctant to fire a kill shot, having never killed a person before.

The town had elected me their captain not knowing they had the great Sitting Bull in their midst. But I would never do anything without consulting him. We knew better then trying a frontal assault. Much like the World War I front, both sides dug in. We had a stand off.

"Any idea? I asked, not just Bull and Annie but the townspeople. Lance Richardson suggested we sneak around the wooded side of town and come at them.

"How much open space after the woods."

"About 30 yards," He replied.

"You really want to take that chance?"

He shrugged leaving it to me.

"No. I don't want any of you hurt or killed if I can help it. Lets keep half on watch and half relax. Lance, can I get you to make two divisions. No kids or mothers, okay?"

"Yes sir," he said and saluted.

"Were you in the military?" I asked him.

"Sir, with the US Cavalry, fought against the Apaches in New Mexico."

Bull laughed, "Those ragtag runaways. Good thing you didn't deal with real fighting Indian tribes.

An hour later Mr. Richardson reported back. "Divisions completed sir. Anything else?"

"Yes Lance, I have an important job for you and one other volunteer. Pick one that can ride."

We slept in the partly dug trench that night. Half on watch for four-hour shifts. Every half hour ten men would fire a round at Smith's group. I didn't want them to feel too comfortable or get much sleep. The next morning there were no white flags. The standoff continued.

Two older men from our ranks had been redcoats in the British army during the Crimean War. They started calling the town Smith's Sebastopol after the Russian stronghold that endured a long siege. Soon, we all started calling the town Sebastopol.

The routine was getting almost too routine. An attack could take place at any time. I had to keep my people alert. So, I met with Bull and we planned a raid.

I wanted all the kerosene and oil lanterns we could get. I sent logger Cliff Sanders and farmer Tim Brown to skirt around behind our foes using the forest as cover, while we tried to occupy Smith's attention with a feint to their left flank.

We positioned more than half our mass to the right side of the rock anticline and poured in the lead. They responded by moving a Gatling to that side but held their fire for the apparent assault. I wondered if they might be getting low on ammunition. Those guns go through ammo like a herd of elephants in a leaf feeding frenzy.

The fake and raid worked perfectly. Sanders and Brown came back with all the fuel they could, including a couple of gallons of gasoline used in a "modern" gas stove.

The day burned away. Only one more until this Joe Smith was scheduled for a time machine departure and three days until our jump forward. I doubted he would go. What would we do if he did not go. We hadn't even discussed what to do if he didn't go . . . At least I felt the pressure was on Smith because of our raid.

Then, quickly the tables turned. Five wagons of Smith's allies rolled into town like they lived there. Where the hell did they come from? How did they know where Smith and his followers were? He must have set this rendezvous with them before this encounter. Watching with binoculars we saw two more of the rapid fire guns unloaded and lots of ammunition. Seven men and four women were added to their ranks.

I had a bad feeling that they came from San Francisco with the smallpox virus. A box with something very valuable was carefully unloaded and was put inside a rooming house.

Now I was sure. The smallpox wasn't a ruse; it could be a weapon against anyone not inoculated. It would not have been hard to hollow out bullets and fill them with live virus. Smith never did plan to use this virus in 2125. He wanted it for here and now.

If he had planned to look like a hero, by using the virus to save people . . . he might be thinking, if I can't be the hero, I'll be a villain. If men, women and children die . . . no matter; just win. He was a ruthless SOB. This Smith guy was starting to piss me off.

Quickly gathering the townspeople together, I had to ask, "How many of you have never gotten a smallpox shot?" Twenty-one hands went up. "You need to head for Santa Rosa, get the vaccine if they have it. Then if you're brave enough, you can return. That is, of course, if we haven't been driven off. Now scram."

Children left with their parents. That left our numbers, including ourselves, down to twenty men and one special woman. We could go on the offensive against Smith's added men and guns, but we didn't have enough firepower to hold them off for very long.

A rifle rang out, shooting into the rocks. The pox was being delivered in an aerial mist. The Mormons waited a couple hours, and then they attacked, wanting to finish us off before it got too dark. Two new Gatling guns were playing the role of tanks at the end of the first World War, spearheading a drive for our trench.

If smallpox was his ace in the hole, I had one also. Ten pre-made Molotov cocktails: Oil bottles with a wick and filled with gas. Hitting my target was key. Rapid fire guns were raking big chucks of hillside rocks.

Desperate, I used a homemade periscope as a sight, I lit the wick and I tossed my best fastball toward the enemy's toward gun. A whoosh-like explosion followed as it hit the gun perfectly. The three man gun crew ignited in a ball of fire, driven by the gasoline. I almost felt sorry for them, almost.

The other forward Gatling gun retreated quickly. Night was falling on our battlefield. The sunset glowed a red tint. "I don't think they will attack again tonight," I said to Bull.

He nodded agreement. "Nice throw."

"Thanks, I pitched some college ball. It's been a while. Not bad considering I had no time to warm up."

Bull said with a chuckle, "You warm up with that stuff and you would run out of catchers."

The man didn't say much but he had a killer sense of humor. I posted a five man watch but the fog was rolling in. We would have to be doubly vigilant after nightfall.

Annie and I escaped into the fog to share some warmth. She said, "You know if the commanding a small army thing and saving the world don't work out; with that arm, Buffalo Bill may be able use ya'."

"What'd he do with two of you? You don't think I'd go without you?"

She stopped and really looked at me. "There you go, trying to get all mushy on me again."

I wasn't buying that line anymore, but kept quiet and held her tight.

Chapter 12

Rocket Man

The morning fog was thick. Dawn was awakening with early luminescence filtering through the convective moisture making it even more difficult for anyone to see beyond a few feet. I passed the word to be focused, use every sense. We almost expected an attack. I heard something behind us; horses. Were we being flanked? "Guns at the ready, watch your backs," I ordered.

"Don't shoot," I heard Lance Richardson yell. I could barely make him out. He had five Chinese men from San Francisco with him. "You get them?"

"Yes sir." Still the loyal soldier. The Chinese men had a special skill. They crafted firework shows. I had requested the most powerful bottle rockets money could buy. These babies were prime, with lots of TNT. I was about to be a rocket man again.

The Chinese specialists planned the new show carefully, aiming not at the sky but where we last saw the four remaining Gatling guns. If I couldn't get artillery, this was the next best thing. The fog kept the enemy oblivious to my plan.

As soon at the fog cleared enough to see the enemy's gun emplacements, I attacked, firing rockets constantly at each gun. "Fire at will," I ordered. With the rockets blasting their camp, Smith's group could not hold the line. Most took off running for the hills. I had no desire to pursue and cut them down.

It was Joe Smith that I had to catch or kill. His troops abandoned him but he kept shooting. Annie had no qualms about sending the Mormon to his heaven . . . or hell, more likely. Smith ran at us past the exploding rockets, two six-shooters blazing like he was in one of those old Western Hollywood movies. Annie put a bullet between his eyes.

She spat out, "Say hello to the devil for me."

***

The Battle of Sebastopol was over. The townspeople trickled back in as they heard about the end of the fighting.

Bull turned to me and said, "You're no Crazy Horse, but not bad for a white man. That fireworks thing was a good idea."

"Thank you, we work well together."

"That's what Crazy Horse said."

"You know, a great American said, 'Never judge a man by the color of his skin.'"

"Okay, you did a good job for a *blue eyes.*"

I laughed. "Martin Luther King you're not." I turned serious, "I do worry that we changed history."

Annie said, "Maybe this little town was going to be called Sebastopol anyway."

I gave her a look that said; really?

"It could happen," she said, sarcastic smile on her pretty face.

"Yeah and turtles fly," I said.

Then the real Cavalry arrived.

I had sent the second volunteer to the Presidio in San Francisco for help. Colonel Tom Willis, seeing everything was in control, decided he didn't want to do the paperwork. "This is a civilian matter."

He looked over at Sitting Bull, recognition in his eyes. He had fought against the Sioux. "Aren't you Sitting Bull?"

"No, colonel, he is my friend and a member of the local Mayacama tribe. Everyone knows Sitting Bull is traveling back east in Buffalo Bill's Wild West Show.

Sitting Bull said to me, "The one and only time I would want to see the US Army . . . they show up when it's too late." He shook his head sadly.

Chapter 13

The Spy

"Annie, I don't want to go back to 2125," I said, "where those non-human big-headed things run the world. It's a world that doesn't have a place for *Huckleberry Finn* or *The Raven* or even Buffalo Bill and Annie Oakley. They would take away both your sex organs and mine."

"Couldn't we could join the Renegades and keep our guns?" Annie said.

"Sweetness, you spent a lot more time in 2125 than me. How long do you think they would leave us alone? How long would they let the girl who is all woman, who can do anything better than . . . I know you hate the 'mushy stuff' so I'll just tell you straight out—I'm in love with you."

"Shucks Dave, come here." Annie pulled me to her and kissed me with a passion that did all the talking for her.

"So, what do you think?" I finally asked.

"Heck, this time period's home to me. If I never see another of those big-headed things again, it would suit me just fine."

"Good, let's go get Bull and tell him what we're thinking."

***

Bull listened to our plan to stay here in this time.

"Won't work," he said.

"Why not?" I asked.

"Remember why they outlawed the time machine? They were afraid that people from the future would come back and change history."

"Yeah Bull, but we wouldn't do that."

"You think they would take that chance?" Bull asked.

"But if we take off their tracking device belts, they couldn't find us."

"They'll know where we are soon enough."

"How?" I asked.

"I've been followed by other tribes and the US Cavalry all my life. I'm pretty good at knowing when someone's tracking me. And someone's been on our trail since Ogden."

"Holy crap! What . . . why didn't you tell us?" I asked.

Annie instinctively looked out the window for the spy.

"I figured you had enough to worry about, Dave. It didn't matter if someone from 2125 was spying on us . . . until you told me you don't want to go back! That caught me by surprise. I was just planning how I was going to shake him."

"Then you don't want to go back either?" Annie said.

"That world is worse than Custer," Bull said.

"You know, I was enjoying a nice relaxing day with no major problems, just planning to invite my girlfriend to have a quiet dinner and watch the sunset. It would have been my first normal ole' day on earth since I was shot into space. Oh well, let's get to it. Any ideas?"

"Yeah," Bull said, "I had it all planned, before you came in. Didn't think an astronaut would want to live in a world without flying machines. You're not so good with a horse."

"Okay, point taken. But choose between this past and that future I'll take the one that makes babies the old-fashioned way."

"Here's my thinking," Bull said. "We turn the tables and capture the spy."

Annie said, "Now you're talkin'. Let's git the bastard."

* * *

Capturing the spy was as easy as pie. Maybe that was the wrong metaphor, since none of us had ever made a pie.

Bull had slyly been watching him watching us, never giving the spy a hint that he was outed. So Annie and I walked down a busy dirt road in Santa Rosa, holding hands but dodging horses and buggies. We never looked at him as we walked past. At a distance, the spy followed us.

Bull followed him, cougar-like, closing in on his prey. At a preplanned spot we stopped. Annie drew her gun, pointing it right at him. The spy knew he was discovered.

But he knew she wouldn't shoot him right
there in the street. He waved with a cocky smile,
but before he could move, the cougar pounced.
Bull had a knife to his throat. He knew Bull
would, if need be, cut right through his jugular.
Surrender he did.

###

Sorry, I need to call a time out from the story to explain something. I already told you I don't fully understand Einstein's theory of relativity, that E=MC squared thing. Remember, I'm not a physicist, never even took a class. So if you're a physicist and think my explanation is subpar, do your job and please explain it better.

The first part of Einstein's theory is easier to explain. Matter is equal to energy on an atomic scale. If you can convert all the atoms of a piece of matter, like uranium, it would make an incredible amount of energy, hence the atomic bomb.

The second part is trickier. Time is relative to the speed at which matter travels. If you can break matter down to the atomic level and send it at the speed of light, the matter can go back in time. Then you put the matter back together and, voila, you have a time machine. Understand? No? Well, neither do I. That's why he was Einstein, I'm me and you are you.

Now can we get back to the story?

* * *

The spy's name was Jack Youngman. Tied up in Bull's room, he showed no reluctance to answering our questions. At this point, he really had nothing to hide.

He told us he was sent through the time machine shortly after we were. His assignment was to report everything in a written journal. He was to leave that journal in a specially designed bag buried in the grave marked Marie Sandman.

He completed that task yesterday, so the Corporation Board in 2125 went to the grave, dug it up, read Youngman's journal and knew about our successful mission so far. Youngman actually smiled after he told us, like he was proud to give the future the good news.

"Did you watch the battle?" I asked.

"Of course. That was the best; the three of you were amazing."

"We could have used your help," I said.

"That wasn't my job. They were very specific. I was just to watch."

"What are you doing for the Big Heads now?" Bull asked.

"Just watching. I'm supposed to watch you put on the transmission belts and depart on the wave from the time machine. I am to follow you an hour later. I understand why you are upset with my spying on your mission. But you did what they wanted. The epidemic will soon be over. You will get a big bonus."

I shook my head. "You don't understand the whole deal do you? We only figured it out in the last few days. The sixties super virus isn't killing the Mods -- because if they knew about it they would already have built-in immunity. The virus is killing you, the Renegades. The Big Heads have total control of the time machine. They didn't need us to attack this lunatic. They sent him here."

"They sent a clone of Joe Smith here and another one to get the sixties super virus. They knew they were safe from those two viruses. They genetically engineered their immunity while starting a well-aimed epidemic. They are going to get rid of all the Renegades; you included."

"What about their built-in morality?" Youngman asked.

"To them, we're not human anymore. That bypasses their morality. Just like when the British came to America and traded blankets with smallpox to the Indians to kill them off. To the British, the Indians were subhuman."

"So why did they send us here?" asked the spy.

"That's what we were wondering about, why did they send us? We came to two conclusions: First, to make it look like they were doing something to kill the epidemic and we also think we were sent here for their entertainment," I answered. "They wanted to see what we could do. Probably put bets on each of us like the old Kentucky Derby."

Bull added, "If we go back to 2125, they won't set us free. They probably have another amusing assignment for us, even more dangerous."

"So, what will you do?" Jack wondered.

"Why would we be telling you that?" Annie told him. "I think a better question is, what are you going to do?"

"I've got to go back. My wife and two kids are there."

"Tell you what we can do. We have all the vaccine that was brought back to Smith. It would be a good idea if you didn't tell them about this meeting and what we know about them. I'm not sure this vaccine will really work against the super virus but let's give it a shot. We'll vaccinate you right now and bury the rest of the virus near Joe Smith's grave. The graves will be marked with the names: Dave O'Brien, Bull Lakota, and Ann Oak. That should provide a great many of the Renegades in the future with the vaccine."

"That's really nice of you, Mr. O'Brien."

"Actually, I'm not that nice. It was Annie's idea. Tell them you never saw us after you turned in your report. Now git," I said, in the local vernacular.

"Thank you all. You may have saved our lives."

Bull said, "Yeah, get the hell out of here before we change our minds."

Chapter 14

Go East Young People

We went to lunch on Santa Rosa Avenue at a joint that had a sign that said, "Good Food." Annie picked it. She said, "They wouldn't lie."

I said, "Get the stomach pump ready."

Annie giggled. Bull frowned.

After we were seated and served with what actually looked to be a good home cooked meal, I said, "We have a lot of decisions to make. Annie, will you come with me?"

"Was that some kind of proposal? Aren't you supposed to get down on one knee?"

"Sorry babe, can't attract that much attention. Besides, you don't like mushy stuff."

"Hey, a girl can change her mind, can't she?"

"You will just have to wait till I get you alone."

Bull said, "You two are ruining my appetite."

"Okay, you know I want to go wherever you're going," Annie said to me.

Just then a couple walked by and did a double-take. "You're Annie Oakley, aren't you. Can I get an autograph?"

Bull growled, "No, she is not. Annie Oakley is with the Buffalo Bill's Wild West Show in New York. Now go away."

I said, "Bull, you know you're so charming, you should look for a job in sales. Maybe at a used buggy showroom. But seriously, we can't call you Annie anymore and as much as I love your hair, you've got to change the color. That flaming red is a sure giveaway. How 'bout I just call you Suzie? Bull, what do you want to do?"

He said, "I can't go to my tribe. The real Sitting Bull is touring with Buffalo Bill. If you don't mind, I'll just tag along with you."

I looked at Ann. . . uh, Suzie. She smiled and nodded. "Guess we're still a team."

"Okay, we need to leave right now, after we bury the vaccine and pay for the headstones. We also need to change the money the Mods made for our trip. Bull, you need a new name too. Time to hit the banks, then hit the road. Any ideas where to go?"

Bill and A . . . Suzie just looked at me.

"How 'bout New York, not city but state. Ever heard of Irvington? Named after Washington Irving, the author, you know, *The Headless Horseman*? I always thought the town sounded nice, right on the Hudson River."

Suzie said, "I didn't read it, but some boy would always dress like that horseman every Halloween."

I laughed, thinking about *Rip Van Winkle*, who fell asleep and woke up many years later, kind of like what I did. Did Washington Irving know about time travel? No, couldn't be . . . could it? Nah, I'm . . . oh well, who knows? I tried to let that idea go.

"Sorry, my mind took a walk," I said. "I don't think we should go anywhere we've been before. They know our history and will send people there. I think they think we would stay in the West. Bull you and I need a name change also. I'll go by Dave York. Bull, how 'bout Bill Chairman? Get it? Chairman, as in Sitting?"

Bull/Bill said, "Yes Dave, very funny." But he would not even show me the courtesy of a smile. The newly named Suzie at least chuckled.

The former Annie Oakley asked, "Spaceman, you never told me. Where are you from?"

I sang the first line badly, "I left my heart in San Francisco."

Chapter 15

A Century Turns

We travelled an unusual route east. Took the train as far as Utah. Once across the desert, we travelled in an old covered wagon east to St. Louis. Hopped another train to Pittsburgh and made the final trek on horseback to Irvington, our destination.

We were happy. It was the happiest time of my life. For six years, Suzie and I lived a normal turn-of-the-twentieth-century life. I taught high school history. Annie/Suzie became the fittest housewife north of New York City. She, of course, took hours of target practice every day. I know she wanted to join the suffrage movement but that would draw undue attention.

I loved her and we were lovers. I couldn't get enough of her. I found myself thinking of her during the day between classes, when I was on playground duty.

The town and countryside were quite lovely. Our house had a clear view of the Hudson, with cliffs staring back at us across the river. You couldn't imagine the colors in autumn. It was like God took out a paint brush, attacking every last leaf. But growing up in San Francisco, I thought the New York winters were harsh.

In the spring of 1894 Suzie joined the flights of birds and bees hovering about the multitude of flowers in this fertile landscape. She told me joyfully that she was with child. Nine months later we had our first baby, William Lakota York, but everyone called him Willie.

Baby Ann was born in the winter of 1897. She had a crop of red hair and looked very much like her mother. As proud parents, we were overjoyed.

I asked Suzie, "You ever get sad that you never got to play Annie Oakley in the Wild West show?"

"She should be jealous of me. While she was fightin' make believe battles against Indians, I fought the very real Battle of Sebastopol. I also got the battle's leading man."

"Ah, Suzie you're not getting all mushy on me, are you?"

Bill Chairman was always around. He rented the place next door. He did odd jobs and sold his paintings for a living. His Dakota landscapes were always in demand.

I engaged in writing a very special history of the United States, but it was about the future not the past. It was for the York family to read, no one else. It was the same thing with this journal.

So far, we had not a sign from the Mods of the future. We didn't even know if they were still after us. We settled into a very normal life. One evening, we invited Bill over for dinner.

Mr. Chairman said, "I don't think we will change history in our quiet little neck of the world."

"We already did that at the Battle of Sebastopol."

"I have a bad feeling about tomorrow," Bill said.

"What do you think will happen?" Annie asked.

"I have no idea and it bothers me."

"Your Lakota spirits are talking?" I asked.

"Yeah, and not very well, because I don't think I'm the one in danger."

"Well let me know if they tell of anything important."

Bill knew I was making a little fun of him. I didn't believe in spirits talking but I didn't totally disbelieve. I've heard and seen stranger things, like time machines.

*****

Over these last few years the Big Heads sent twenty-two Renegade spies to look for us. They always picked married guys they believed would come back, if not for the safety of their family, for the high salary paid by the Mods. Also, a great reward for the one who found us, dead or alive. Each of them knew if they did not return, a bounty would go on their head.

But the bounty hunters came as strangers in this strange world. Some made rudimentary progress but it would seem we covered our tracks and left few clues to uncover. Each agent returned unsuccessfully. One found our grave site but after digging up each grave no bodies were discovered. "Just a ruse," he said to himself. The vaccine was rescued long before the graveyard exploration.

***

Okay now you're wondering how in the world I know this. No fairies or ghosts told me. Do you remember Jack Youngman? He was the spy and follower of our 1893 adventure. He came back, used the time machine to get here. His arrival sure shocked the heck out of me.

103

He had an amazing story to tell and brought along a revised history book of the future. You know I teach history, so I read the whole thing twice. I put this future in my family journal. I decided to tell only the parts needed to get the whole picture of what the future may bring. It is truly amazing.

I will call this history book: Past the Future, Part Two.

Past the Future

Part II

Style note:

I'm going to tell this account, not like a history book, but as a non-fictional story. Since it took place mostly without me, I'll now switch to third person. Okay? Bye for now.

Chapter 16

Ford and Mitsubishis

Dave and Susie York did not change history. They had two children, William and Ann. William, their son, married a local girl after college with the last name of Rockefeller. Yes, the family of John D. Rockefeller who owned Standard Oil. Unfortunately, William, assigned to an English unit during World War I, was declared missing in action.

Will's sister, Ann, married a Ford, the family of Henry Ford, largest car builder in America.

Ann now had wealth, power and connections. Ann Ford had a son,

David, who graduated from Yale in 1939. The young man enjoyed flying his latest airplane around the country. Ann's second child, a girl, was named Susan, after her grandma.

When the Japanese bombed Pearl Harbor, David Ford figured he had two choices, Navy or Army. He liked the blue uniform; matched his eyes. Since he could already fly, they fast-tracked him to staff duty in D.C..

Friends of Henry wanted to keep the young Mr. Ford safe. To his credit, David wanted to fight and used his influence to get assigned to a dive bomber squadron on the USS Enterprise just in time for the Battle of Midway.

David arrived aboard the aircraft carrier by plane, delivered with the airmail right to the flight-deck. Usually pilots didn't join a squadron at sea but these were not normal times. Ford had qualified on dive bombers and fighters. Bomber Squadron Nine had lost men, injured and killed in the Coral Sea engagement with the enemy.

He joined two other rookies newly assigned to the squadron. He brought his sea bag below to his quarters. Beds hung like hammocks, four high. Not an inch of space could be wasted.

Fully loaded with air squadrons, the Big E, the ship's nickname, held thousands of sailors. Tim Stafford didn't look up from his book when Ford said, "Hello." He hadn't noticed that after Ford lay his big bag on a rack (the name for beds aboard ship) that David picked up five tennis balls and starting juggling.

"I'm right at the good part, be with you in a minute." Lt. Stafford finally looked up at the newbie. "What the hell are you doing Ford? That's your name, right?"

"Yes Ford, sir, I'm juggling. They say flying in combat is like juggling five things at a time, so I'm practicing."

"Well, it couldn't hurt, but don't tell me you haven't been in combat."

"Okay, sir, I won't tell you."

"Great. When we take off, just stick close till the bombing run. Understood? And forget the lieutenant thing, I'm Stafford like everyone else. Only the C.O. is Major Ryan."

"Yes sir, sorry that was from habit. But we'll get into combat, tomorrow morning."

"How could you possibly know that?"

Ford gave a knowing smile and said,

"Let's just say I read ahead."

Stafford said. "You're going to be a strange one, aren't you.

"No, I don't think so, well, maybe a little."

*＊＊

The next morning at first light the scout planes were launched; normal procedure. About an hour later the loudspeaker erupted: "General Quarters, General Quarters, all squadrons, condition Delta, all pilots to the ready room."

Stafford gave Ford a funny look as their planes were elevated to the flight deck to be loaded.

"Did you read any further ahead Ford?"

"Sorry, I don't want to ruin the story for you," Ford said with laughter.

Stafford felt even more uncomfortable than normal. Ford just gave him a thumbs up.

The adrenaline flowed during takeoff; the squadron settled in for the long flight to where the Japanese fleet was spotted, maximum range. Suddenly, up ahead, appeared to be the whole Japanese fleet. Ford saw the skies were devoid of enemy fighters. They were down at sea level after fighting off a torpedo bomber attack.

"Okay this is it," Major Ryan said into the microphone. "Line up and follow me."

David dove right behind Stafford. The Japanese were caught refueling their bombers. Stafford's bomb missed just to starboard but Ford, like his grandma, never missed. His bomb hit the flight deck covered with fuel. The explosion rocked his plane as he pulled out of the dive. Each plane that followed added to the Japanese ships' destruction. Other squadrons were having similar success.

Ford flew another attack before the day ended. He hit and damaged a Japanese cruiser. The Battle of Midway was the greatest American naval success in history and the turning point of the war in the Pacific. David Ford was awarded his first medal.

Chapter 17

Snakes in the Garden of Eden

Ford requested a transfer to a fighter squadron. He felt that was where the glamour was, you know, the Red Baron... and the idea of becoming an Ace.He was transferred to a squadron flying close support for the embattled marines at Guadalcanal.

After a Japanese naval victory, the Battle of Savo Island, the Navy fleet retreated and left the American Marines to fend for themselves. The Marines were up against experienced divisions of Japanese soldiers being reinforced by the ships sneaking down "the slot." The marines knew they somehow had to hold Henderson Airfield as it came under attack after attack.

Ford and the other Navy and Marine pilots rose to the challenge blasting the enemy from the air. Ford was becoming legendary, going up in his beat-up, shot-up fighter plane day after day.

One day his luck ran out. The overworked plane's engine was blasted from ground fire. The plane sputtered and the engine was dead. Ford steered the resulting heavy glider to an opening in the jungle along the beach. It hit the ground hard.

Both the Japanese and Americans battled to the beach to capture or save the pilot. Ford struggled out of the cockpit and sprinted towards the thick plant cover, armed with only a pistol. A squad of Japanese were the first to him and he dived into a thicket as deadly lead whizzed by him.

He felt a burning sensation in his upper leg. He rolled to his belly, took aim, and before you could say Annie Oakley five shots spit from his handgun. Five Japanese fell, blood oozing from holes between their eyes.

Three marines approached from his right. "Lt. Ford, this way," a marine called. Ford struggled to stand and move toward them but his right leg buckled. A big marine slung him over his shoulder and carried the pilot away. They knew the Japs would be on them any second. (I know Jap is a racist term and I normally wouldn't use it, but during that war that's what the Americans called the enemy, so go with it.) The three dragged and carried Ford away, back toward the airfield and across the uncertain American line.

A corpsman attended to the wound in David's thigh leaving the bullet alone, applying sulfur, peroxide and bandages. "How is the pain sir?" the medic asked, "do you want morphine?"

"Shit no," came the answer. "How am I supposed to shoot straight on morphine?" He grabbed a rifle from a dead marine. One of his rescuers looked at him and said, "Did the navy teach you how to use that?"

"We all know they are going to attack and it would appear my plane is unavailable."

The Japs came at them all night in waves. The marines threw all their fire power at each charge. In the morning, thousands lay dead in front of the line.

Another night, they held the field. A plane landed, supplies quickly unloaded and some wounded boarded. Ford didn't want to go but a bird colonel told him, "Shut it."

He was lifting off minutes later.

Chapter 18

Marines Tend to Exaggerate

The Doctor said, "Lt. Ford, you're a lucky man. Here's the bullet that hit your leg. It hit the femur, cracked it, then stopped. You want to keep it?"

"Sure, I think I earned it."

"I guess so. You've been the scuttlebutt of the hospital. Word is you shot five Japs with a pistol. Then, while wounded and on your belly you fired a rifle all night. The jarhead next to you says you never missed, must have killed a hundred Japs, maybe more."

"Well, you know how marines exaggerate."

"True enough for the colonel to put you in for a silver star. They say it's the best shooting since Sergeant York during World War I. You heard about him, lived in the country and hunted. Is that how you learned?"

"Nope, but the legend in my family is that my grandma could out-shoot Annie Oakley."

***

The Oakland Naval Hospital was filled with thousands of wounded. It was not a place for the faint of heart. Men screamed in anguish. Morphine was the only drug that could relieve some of the pain, creating thousands of addicts. Many lay dying, crying for their mothers.

David Ford's sister, Susie, a freshman at Stanford, recruited friends to candy stripe and visited wounded combat veterans. She came to see her brother and went from bed to bed, holding hands and kissing cheeks, to bring cheer to the wounded and battle worn.

It was on one of these visits that she met John F. Kennedy, recovering from a back injury during the sinking of PT 109. It would be the beginning of their unusual relationship.

Susan Ann Ford was given the name of her grandmother and inherited her flaming red hair, green eyes and fiery disposition. She and Kennedy started dating, which turned into a torrid love affair. His good looks, boyish attitude and dry sense of humor attracted her, like, well like two young people, excited in first true love.

Chapter 19

FDR Offers a New Deal

When healthy enough, Ford was sent on a war bonds tour and was awarded the Silver Star and Navy Cross at a special ceremony in the nation's capital. President Franklin Delano Roosevelt pinned the newly made Commander and asked, "Just between you and me, did you really shoot all those Japanese?"

"I had to Mr. President, they just kept coming."

The president chuckled. "Well good shooting, son. Tell me, I know your family, you're a war hero now, do you have any interest in politics?"

"Never gave it much thought."

"Well think about it, your Commander in Chief just might need you."

"Yes sir."

David Ford thought about it as he toured the country. Each local paper played up his story. He became almost legendary before the war was over, like Davy Crockett or Annie Oakley.

Hollywood decided that his story would fit with their role as a wartime propaganda machine. The movie, *Time for a Hero*, was rushed to the screen in record time, like a liberty ship, with John Wayne playing David.

His crowds grew bigger, more war bonds sold at each stop. With so many fighting and dying, David wanted to ship out. Get back in the air.

It was the summer of 1944, election year, and FDR wanted a living legend at the Democratic Convention. His ace in the hole. The man didn't get elected president three times without knowing how to play politics.

The President spent July 4th giving out medals and promoting David Ford to Captain.

"I know you want to get back to the war, but I need you for something else. I want you to confer with General Marshall on war strategy and what we should expect worldwide after the war," FDR told Ford.

"I'm leaving to see MacArthur during the convention. I don't want to be in a cat fight about the vice president.

"The southern conservatives don't like Wallace. They are backing a guy from Missouri by the name of Truman. I know nothing about him except he's a good man, but boring as watching water boil."

"How could they say no to a young good looking war hero; start using your middle initial. When the press asks you what it stands for, tell them liberty."

It took David a full minute to realize FDR just told him he would be the next Vice President of The United States.

The convention took place at the end of July. Ike had taken Normandy and American and British armies were freeing France. The stubborn Japanese resistance was being overwhelmed by US industrial might.

The nomination of FDR to run for a fourth term was a foregone conclusion. Vice President was the delegate voters' choice.

The voting was almost a re-creation of the division of states during the Civil War. Truman was solidly backed by the Dixiecrats and Vice President Wallace backed by the north and east.

"Lay low," the president had told him. "My people know what to do when the time comes."

For the delegates it looked to be quite a battle between the two candidates that would go on for hours, each side trading and making deals all night long.

Suddenly a group of delegates from New York pulled out signs for a new candidate. A leading delegate called, "Mr. Chairman, the Empire State of New York would like to nominate a compromise candidate, a true war hero, David L. Ford."

A small murmur went through the convention floor and grew to a shout. The Chairman asked for a second, "Do I hear a second?"

"Mr. Chairman the great state of Illinois seconds." Speeches were made. The second ballot voting commenced. It was no contest; with FDR's quiet prearranged backing, David won on the first roll-call vote.

The delegates never expected to nominate David L. Ford for Vice President but surprisingly they did just that. Everyone wanted to vote for a war hero, any war hero. FDR provided the right man at the right time.

Chapter 20

The Captain Marshalls a General

It was one of those late August, muggy New York nights. David was already on the campaign trail, having spent a full day going to veteran and union halls in New York City.

The local and national press was his constant companion. Without letting anyone know, he snuck out of the Waldorf's back door and caught a train to Irvington. The family estate was his destination, to meet with his little sister before she left for California and her sophomore year at Stanford.

They relished their time alone together. They had both been away and their relationship was evolving from big brother and little scamp to one of respected adults.

Dave quickly realized how brilliantly his sister's mind worked. He brought up the time he spent with General George Marshall.

"Marshall plans for everything and has a true world view. Ike, McArthur and even Patton get all the press and credit, but without Marshall's careful planning and distribution of equipment, the others would not be winning this two front war.

"Marshall also worries about the political battles after the war. A powerful Russian bear in central Europe gives him the creeps."

"What does FDR think?"

"FDR is a great politician. He is also a pragmatist and delegator. He told me, "I let the George Marshalls figure out how to deal with the future. I'll deal with winning one war at a time.""

"Well, big brother, seems like those two are giving you great advice about opposite sides of the same coin," Susie said with a smile, green eyes flashing.

"I'm so glad I came to see you up here in the fresh air. I'd be tossing and turning in bed in that city hotel room. This is nice."

"You still peeking ahead in that history book Grandpa gave you?"

"Yeah, but now I've taken Truman's spot, it would seem like all bets are off. That book is probably toast."

"Don't look for specifics, big brother. Trends -- look for trends. And from what you've just told me, listen to General George Marshall."

"I'm realizing I'm going to need one more person's advice. Would it be too much for your country to ask that you transfer from Stanford to Georgetown?" he said with a smile. "Maybe two Fords equal a Lincoln.

Susie laughed, then thought about his proposition. "You know, I might even like it in Washington. I'm having fun with Jack Kennedy."

"I'm certainly not the one to give love advice, but the scuttlebutt is that Kennedy is a bit of a rascal."

"Shucks, Davy, that's why I like him," she said, sounding a lot like her grandmother Annie Oakley/Suzie.

Chapter 21

He Read Ahead

Right after the election, Vice President David Ford made his first important executive decision. Its boldness was shrouded in secrecy. He didn't tell the president or anyone else in the administration.

He privately sent a top secret military communique to General Eisenhower:

"General, certain friends in the intelligence community have learned that Hitler is going to make a crazy gamble. He is already amassing tanks and troops for a December attack into Belgium, splitting the English and American forces.

He actually believes he can drive your army back during bad weather when our planes can't dominate. I know you believe this unlikely.

You have had scouts out and aerial reconnaissance and have found no evidence that the German army will attack. Take another look at the Ardennes." Signed, VP-elect Ford. PS -- This stays between you and me. The President is not sure about the intel and wants deniability.

Ike could not ignore this possibility. He sent out scout planes that found little evidence of a possible German attack. Still, he couldn't risk ignoring the cable. He ordered Patton's First Army to move north, to be a reserve for the front lines.

When Hitler made his last gamble, Patton counterattacked, saving thousands of American lives. There was no "Bulge." The battle was now called "The Battle of Bastogne." The Nazi forces surrendered and Patton poured into Germany, changing the East-West borders for the coming Cold War.

***

In late afternoon of April 12, 1944, the radio announcer interrupted the music.

"We have a special bulletin announcement: President Franklin Roosevelt is dead. He was with his family when he passed on. His death was due to natural causes. Again, President Roosevelt is dead."

The country mourned the man who had governed America longer than any other President. He saw the country through a terrible Depression and led them to the brink of victory in a desperate war.

David was sworn in as President and the shocked nation did not believe the young man was ready to fill FDR's shoes. No cameras were allowed at the swearing-in, just a simple press release.

After President Ford paid his respects to FDR, he made three important gestures. First, he boarded a train to Missouri and asked Truman to be his Vice President. That helped shore up Dixiecrat support. But he also needed Truman's help for a plan he had for postwar politics.

David was single; no first lady. He wanted his sister to fill the role and be a member of his staff, but knew she'd be viewed by the public as too young. He asked Eleanor Roosevelt to stay in that role and take Susie under her wing while she continued college at Georgetown. His approval rating immediately jumped.

He needed the extra approval points for his next plan. FDR had trusted Stalin too much and Ford knew the Soviet dictator would be a problem. Japan expected invasion. David stalled the Pacific troops.

While the Russians blasted to and through Berlin, he had Patton do an end run and liberate Czechoslovakia. Then he had McArthur invade Korea using the same plan used at **Inchon** that could prevent the future Korean War.

Stalin protested at both invasions but realized he was outmaneuvered. When Hitler killed himself and Germany surrendered, British and American troops were just outside the gates of Berlin.

With Korea now tucked in his pocket, Ford changed the game on Japan. He offered them an honorable surrender. They could keep the Emperor and get back Okinawa, in time, if they surrendered.

If they did not accept this proposal, Ford would go back to the plan of unconditional surrender. He gave them a week to "capitulate with honor," as he called it, and stopped the bombing for a week.

The powerful warlords still had control of the Japanese government. They wavered and decide to fight on. It took only one atomic bomb for the Emperor to intervene and order a surrender. That bomb also convinced Russia not to interfere in Korea. The U. S. celebrated V-J day with a stronger postwar poker hand.

Chapter 22

Israel is Real

The press called the young president, Davy Ford. He liked it; being a man of the people like Davy Crockett. With the war over, he was the most powerful and popular figure in the world. He was able to use his popularity politically.

Senator Joe McCarthy had started his rabid anti-communist campaign to attack liberals, progressives and union workers. President Ford decided to nip this unpleasant black rose in the bud.

He invited McCarthy to come see him and new Secretary of State George Marshall for cocktails at the White House. He got right to the point.

"Senator McCarthy, you are saying some nasty things about my government and some of my friends, calling them Commies and such.

You are aware that Franklin Roosevelt met with Stalin during World War II; that Russia was America's ally? That President Roosevelt started the social program called the New Deal to get us out of the Great Depression? Are you going to call FDR a Commie?"

"Of course not, Mr. President, I'm talking about real Communists."

"Okay, that could be important. Let me have your list of 'real' Communists."

"We . . . the list is incomplete, we are still assessing . . .

"That's not what you said in the Senate, so let's cut to the chase. Unless you want my foot up your butt and to have Wisconsin frozen out of government contracts, you will stop this nonsense and let the FBI do its job."

"Mr. President you wouldn't . . .

"Listen, you overgrown bully, I've seen waves of Japanese soldiers come at me. You don't even blip my radar. If you continue this nonsense you'll start to wish you were sitting next to Joe Stalin. Now, senator, is there anything my staff can get you on your way out?"

"No, Mr. President."

"Excellent."

After the Senator left, David turned to Marshall and said, "I think that went well."

"You can be very intimidating, Mr. President; remind me to keep on your good side. Now, are you ready to meet the press to announce our two big international plans?"

"I haven't been this nervous since Midway," David said.

They came out of the Oval Office to the press room. President Ford stepped up to the podium.

First, Ford announced the Marshall Plan to use American aid to rebuild postwar Europe and fight Communist influence. Then he presented a plan to change history.

"I am embarrassed and ashamed that the United States and the other countries of the world did not do more to help the Jews during the war.

"What was uncovered in the concentration camps"… He shook his head and raised his arms, "Unbelievably inhuman. I understand why Zionists want a homeland in Palestine."

"That is not possible for two reasons. If a Palestinian homeland is established, the surrounding countries will find it unacceptable and the hostility could go on indefinitely, creating worldwide instability."

"What should we do about the Jewish refugee problem? I propose we open our doors and our hearts. The United States under my plan will accept any Jewish refugee that wants entry. These peoples will not be a burden but an asset to our country, like the Jews who immigrated earlier.

Remember, my fellow Americans, the Statue of Liberty: 'Give me your tired, your poor, your huddled masses yearning to breathe free. Send these, the homeless tempest-tossed to me'. I am proud to be part of this legacy. Thank you. God bless America."

With the Ford policy, there was no state of Israel founded on Palestinian land in the Middle East. It saved a lot of trouble with the Arab states. In total some three million Jewish refugees spilled into the United States. Most went to big cities on the East Coast and in California.

A large group settled in western Arizona and eastern California along the Colorado River. They called the town, New Jerusalem. They established an amazing irrigation system, years ahead of its time, using the world's first drip system. The settlement thrived.

They built a great temple and Hebrew became their second language. The area grew and in1951, New Jerusalem and its surrounding area became the 49th state; the state's name was Israel.

Chapter 23

Not Only Bills Die in The Senate

Isaac Cohen, a Jew who grew up in Palestine, hated David Ford. He lost his dream when Ford turned his back on the Zionists.

Who was Ford to decide where a Jewish homeland could be? God gave us Palestine, he thought. No one had the right to give up the Jewish land, the land of David, the King, not David the president.

Expelled from his land by local Arabs, his resentment turned to hate.

Isaac came to the United States to recruit a Zionist army. Failing that, he founded a group of followers that was going to . . . they weren't sure yet.

The FBI had them in their sights. Then the close-knit group of ten, who called themselves the Minion, disappeared into the vast lands of the United States.

***

The president met with his new secretary of defense, Dwight Eisenhower. Ike felt indebted to David for having warned him about Hitler's surprise December attack.

Having seen the German Autobahn firsthand, Ike expressed how much it helped military mobilization and suggested a similar Interstate Highway system in the United States. David agreed and the auto industry rejoiced.

"What is good for General Motors is good for America," came out of the chairman of that company's mouth. President Ford smiled at the disdain that GM's boss showed for his family's auto company. But it was something else that the car industry did, something that made a small change to the nation at the time, that would set a big legal precedent for the future.

A group of oil tycoons, auto barons and tire company CEOs bought up street car lines in big cities and started to tear them down. To the total surprise of this conglomerate, the president intervened on the side of the street cars. He sued Detroit and the conglomerate under the long disused Sherman Anti-Trust Act. A federal court judge ordered an injunction.

He was a Ford, for gosh sake, thought the conglomerate's monied interests. Why would he do this? His simple answer was there was plenty of room for both cars and city streetcars.

The legal precedent made it much harder for illegal conglomerates of companies to work together, just as Teddy Roosevelt had envisioned, the Sherman Anti-Trust Act would work for the common man.

***

As the election of 1950 approached, the Dixiecrats in congress made it known that they were not too happy with President Ford. They especially opposed the free Jewish immigration and the racial integration of the military, even if it was backed by Vice President Truman.

Ford proposed a meeting in the Senate chambers. The Minion showed up just after the president. They walked past the unassuming guards and up to the gallery, pistols tucked neatly in sport coat pockets. When the president came into view, Bruce Levy, the best sharpshooter of the group, took aim. Just before he could fire, Levy was blasted by a Secret Service agent.

Chaos reigned. Senators hid behind their desks as a frantic firefight broke out between the Minion and the Secret Service men and an almost useless poorly-trained group of Senate guards.

Three of the Minion assault team avoided the Secret Service and guards to make their way onto the Senate floor. They took out two Secret Service men and were closing in on the seemingly defenseless Senate leaders and the President.

Davy had been warned about this group months back, by the FBI. When they disappeared from the agents' investigation, the president felt personally threatened. He started packing heat in a holster under his coat jacket and practiced shooting with Secret Service agents.

Davy drew his gun like his grandmother, Annie Oakley. Three blasts rang out from his 45 automatic and three Jewish fanatics lay bleeding on the senate floor, each with a bullet between the eyes.

Chapter 24

The Bride and Her Two Playboys

The American people were dismayed by how close the fanatical group got to the President in the Senate chambers. Yet they were awed by and proud of their elected leader. Their heroic president was once again a hero. Nothing in Hollywood could compare to the real thing.

Not one Dixiecrat Senator or Congressman voted against the post war integration of the military. Some abstained, but no one dared to vote against Ford at the time.

The team of Ford and Ike trounced Douglas MacArthur and Richard Nixon in the 1952 general election.

It was the first and only time that the electoral college of all 49 states voted for one candidate. It was time to free up his old friend Eleanor Roosevelt from her job as fill-in First Lady.

With his unprecedented popularity, Ford named his sister Susan Chief of Staff. Some papers brought up the idea of nepotism, but Davy answered their charges by saying that Susan's years of experience in the White House made her the most qualified. Besides, he said,

"She is a better shot than me."

***

Later that year she married John Fitzgerald Kennedy. It was a fairytale White House wedding. The bride's fiery red hair sparkled as it curled down her snowy white dress. Her happy blue eyes completed the national colors.

Her beauty had every man watching sweet Susie became Mrs. Susan Ford Kennedy, walking up the aisle with such grace; America's sweetheart.

Handsome JFK in his morning coat with tails had the woman's eyes glued to their sets as well. The perfect couple; everyone thought.

***

Ford's second administration was dominated by the Cold War and Civil Rights. Because World War II, in this reality, ended with the Americans just outside Berlin, East Germany was much smaller. There was no need for a Berlin airlift and no wall cutting off East Berlin from the West. There was no Korean War.

China still went Red. Instead of isolating China, Ford sent Ike to meet Mao and offered to let China rule their way as long as they didn't interfere with America's sphere of influence.

Mao did not formally sign any treaties but the two countries unofficial agreement was; stay out of each other's way. That gave Mao a certain independence from Russia. Still, the Russian bear seized the rest of Eastern Europe.

To pacify the big corporate sponsors, David proposed space exploration. The federal funds spent on that project would make the defense industry happy. But they would have to compete for contracts, no conspiring. He appointed his brother-in-law, JFK, to oversee the program.

A US satellite barely beat Russia's Sputnik into space.

David, at the height of his popularity, was only rivaled by Susan and Jack Kennedy who lived in the White House.

Davy was still the bachelor, hanging out with movie stars. Dean Martin, Frank Sinatra and Sammy Davis wanted to be seen with the president.

David dated a parade of famous beauties, including Marilyn Monroe, Sophia Loren, even French temptress Bridget Bardot.

The public could always rely on Susan as the unofficial First Lady. So when she took a job at Stanford in California and left Kennedy, it was a surprise.

When he was with his family in Massachusetts, John was rumored to spend some time with a pretty brunette. Susan could read the writing on the wall. She went right to John and asked if the rumors were true.

He said, "You can't believe what you read in those rags."

"I know that. That's why I'm asking you."

John thought about lying, but he knew it wouldn't work.

She smiled at him. "Thanks for the truth."

Hardly devastated, she felt they were drifting apart in the past months.

The Kennedy-Ford marriage annulment kept the society pages busy.

Chapter 25

A Jefferson Ends David's Declaration of Independence

President David Ford liked his friend Jack Kennedy and kept him on as Space Director with his sister's permission. He told her on the phone "I see your relocation to Stanford as a great opportunity. You'll be your own woman, not a wife or even my sister espousing some man's position. If you play it right, you can run for Senate in '56 and become the first woman president in 1960."

Susie laughed. "Is that what you saw in grandpa's history book? I don't think our nation is ready for a formerly married woman -- who is so out front on civil rights -- as their president."

"Well, I might have some surprises for you on that front, but grandpa's history book has taken some hard hits. I think we've changed history a bit."

"What are you going to do? Appoint Jackie Robinson to the Supreme Court?"

"Not a bad idea, but I think he has enough going on with the Brooklyn Dodgers."

***

The next week David Ford shocked his sister and the rest of the nation by announcing his engagement to a young sexy Washington school teacher. The brunette had big brown eyes and a rich tan. She went by the name of Robin Hemings-Jefferson. Everyone wondered if she had some people of color in her ancestry. She could easily pass as white in the south.

Miss Hemings-Jefferson made it quite clear when the couple was interviewed by Barbara Walters. "I was not given this name at birth. I appropriated it from my ancestors. My great-great-great-grandmother, Sally Hemings, was the lover and slave of the great President, Thomas Jefferson. Both of them are in my DNA. I am very proud of my heritage."

Barbara turned and asked, "Mr. President what do you think about this?"

"I love every part of Robin. All of her will be my wife, and mother to my children."

"What do you think people in the South will say about this?"

"I want to make this perfectly clear. Not all people in the South are bigots. But those who cling to their racism can no longer claim to be one of the good guys. They will go down in history like the Nazis in Germany. Everyone has prejudice, Barbara, but if you want to be on the side of the angels you must fight it with all your heart."

Robin and David met at a White House fundraiser for scholarships for inner-city students; one of hundreds he did each year; normally a fifteen-minute obligation. He heard her laugh before he saw her. It was not a shy laugh, but one that said, "I'm having fun."

David turned and there she was, unlike anyone he'd ever seen. Skin a rich light brown, like an Italian coming from the beach with an olive oil tan. Her long lashes led to sultry brown eyes and rich red lips he knew he wanted to kiss.

She didn't shy away from his gaze like most women faced by the President of the United States. The woman showed a regal confidence. He thought that this must be what Caesar first saw when he encountered Cleopatra. Romance and passion had finally found David Ford.

They were quietly married, inside the White House.

Their honeymoon was spent on the Carolina coast; inviting controversy. The hotel owner did not have the fortitude to tell the presidential party that they could not stay in a white hotel.

The President drank from the colored drinking fountain, the First Lady from the white.

When a local paper asked him about it, President Ford replied with a smirk firmly planted on his face. "A famous Virginian was noted for saying that, 'All men are created equal.' Did I ever mention I had an uncle who was an Indian? Sioux, I believe."

***

The next week Hollywood released a new movie. The President's buddy Dean Martin played the first First Gentleman of the White House. Audrey Hepburn played President Linda Jeffers, former Army nurse.

"Her best work. You could believe she could be president," raved *The New York Times*. (President Ford wasn't listed as the producer.)

***

Around the globe many European powers were willfully or forcefully losing their colonies.

Gandhi became a saintly figure as the British left India. The US tried to set an example, granting Filipino independence. Other places did not transition well. Africa was a mess. In the Middle East, without Israel to blame for their problems, tribal and ancient adversaries fought over parcels of land.

The French refused to give up Indochina without a fight. They were driven out by brilliant Communist leader Ho Chi Minh. Monied interests wanted President Ford to get involved. "That would be a grave mistake," he imparted.

A reporter asked, "Don't you believe in the domino theory, that countries will fall like dominoes to Communism?"

The President said, "I prefer a good game of poker. Never bet good money on un-winnable hands. Besides, it is a fact that the Vietnamese distrust the Chinese more than the French.

"Mark my words, if we negotiate with Ho we will be building resorts there in a few years. I have assurances the Vietnamese will be better friend than foe.

"Besides, the Russians have their own problems with Poland's mass demonstrations for freedom. We will support the Polish people's liberation."

***

Khrushchev was not happy with President Ford. He did his shoe banging number at the United Nations and everybody wondered how the Soviet People left him in charge of nuclear weapons.

The southern politicians and right-wing extremists weren't happy with the president either. How could they coexist with segregation and a colored First Lady in the White House.

Yet they found it difficult to protest his choice of wife, especially a direct descendent of Declaration of Independence writer and Founding Father Thomas Jefferson.

It seemed all so embarrassing, the more progressive ones started thinking that Ford was right. To be a segregationist was not to be on the side of the angels.

It was not an act. Robin and David were in love. They were very aware of the political ramifications of their marriage, so they let it percolate with the American psyche and sense of justice. The reality of change would take time.

Chapter 26

Tall, Dark and Handsome

The two men faced each other on the hot dry dusty street. Both men wore Levi's denim pants. One wore a black shirt and a matching cowboy hat. An ugly red scar, earned in a knife fight, covered his right cheek.

The other man -- who could easily be described as tall, dark and handsome -- sported a white hat and shirt covered with the star of a lawman.

"Drop your guns, Billy," demanded Sheriff Bart Mills.

Billy said, "Sheriff, I ain't goin' to jail."

"You should have thought of that before you robbed the Wells Fargo stage."

Billy went for his gun and quick as lightning, Mills drew and blasted the bad guy.

The lawman calmly walked over, kicked the gun safely away and said, "I wish you didn't draw, Billy."

Billy said, with great effort, "Tell Sally....I love..." He fell silent, dead.

The big sheriff said, "Don't worry Billy, I'll tell Sally." He turned and walked down the hot dusty street.

"CUT!" yelled the director. "Print. Great job everybody."

The tall actor walked over to Susan Ford. "Well, what do you think?"

"You were great, Sam. That was fun."

The name of the show was *Gold and Lead*. Sam Roth was the star. They taped the show in Columbia, California, a historically-preserved Gold Rush town and State Park in the Sierra Nevada Foothills. It was the perfect setting for the show; a TV hit about a lawman during the California Gold Rush.

***

Susan and Sam met a month earlier at the Fairmont Hotel in San Francisco. She was alone, nursing a glass of Napa Cabernet. A friend from her Stanford days had to bail out of their meeting because of a sick daughter. It turned out to be a fortuitous stand-up.

Of course, Sam recognized her and saw she was sitting alone. He thought, what the heck, I've always admired this women from afar, maybe she'll have a drink with me. He approached and was intercepted by two Secret Service agents almost as tall as he. They did a quick search, patting him down as Susan smiled at him and shrugged her shoulders. He smiled back and she waved him over.

"Hi, you're kind of a big boy, aren't you?"

"Six-five," He said automatically.

"I'm Susan, and you are?"

Surprised that she didn't know who he was, he said, "Of course, I know who you are. I'm Sam, Sam Roth."

Looking him up and down, Susan said, "I'll bet you played basketball."

"Yes, in high school, but I'm better known for baseball. I played first base for the Giants for a year."

"Really, you played for New York? I should have known, I've been following the Dodgers these days, you know, Jackie Robinson."

"Yeah, now that I'm not playing, I'm a fan of his too. But I still can't stand the Dodgers."

"I'm sorry if this is a strange question, but why just one year?"

"It's okay, I'm over it. I played first base and tore up the minors. Looked like Superman. Started well in New York but the pitchers in the majors learn quickly if you have a weakness. The major league slider was my kryptonite."

"Sorry, so what do you do now?

Sam smiled a big smile. "I'm an actor."

"Wow, my brother liked to spend time with actors before he was married. I would have remembered you in a movie so I guess I've missed yours."

"Actually, I have a TV show."

"Sorry, I don't get to watch much TV. Is it popular?"

"Yup, top ten. It's a western."

"I guess I'm going to watch some TV," she said with a laugh.

That's how their romance started.

He knew she was the finest women he'd ever met. Two months later, Sam proposed at the top of the Fairmont Hotel.

"Will you be faithful to me?" asked Susan. "I couldn't take another Kennedy."

"I don't want to get you and those Secret Service guys angry. I'm stuck on you, all the way Susan."

" I believe you Sam. I'm lucky to have you. We haven't talked much about this; I know you're not religious, but I'm curious, were your parents Jewish?"

"Yes," he said tentatively.

"Don't worry about it," she laughed to herself. "But as politicians, my brother and I are breaking all the rules."

***

Susan kept her Stanford house when she moved to D.C. She always thought she might need it. It was a place to hide from the limelight every once in a while.

It also made her a California resident in 1958, she ran for the US senate. It was the end of the post war baby boom and a pregnant Susan Ford Roth had the sympathy and the vote of most of the state's women.

Susan ran a campaign calling for great schools and daycare for women who had to work. Her Republican opponent referred to her as, "the little woman" who should just stay home. He did not endear himself to the women voters. Susan won in a landslide.

On the other side of the country, John F. Kennedy won a Senate seat from Massachusetts.

Her victory party was at the Fairmont. David was the first person to call and congratulate her. It was interesting, the way she felt about his call. Almost rancorous. She felt she'd won the election on her own, without needing her big brother. Their father died when they were young, but she always had David, her father figure.

As the evening was ending, there was Sam, sitting with the great Willie Mays, talking baseball, not trying to run her life. She smiled at him across the room with love, and a deep sense of satisfaction.

San Francisco was now major league. California had passed New York as the most populous state. Senator Susan Ford-Ross was also in the big leagues. She was a giant.

Chapter 27

Anything You Can Do

Susan decided to run for president in 1960, after only two years in the senate. Her poll numbers were good and the opposition seemed weak. Richard Nixon, also from California, was frontrunner for the Republicans. But then, inside her own party, her ex-husband John Kennedy, threw his hat in the ring. With his brothers Bobby and Teddy, he would have a first class campaign organization.

She was reluctant to call her brother for help. Sam was insistent, "Current ball players always need coaches who've been there before."

David knew she needed some southern support so he suggested she pick powerful house majority leader Lyndon B. Johnson, to back her. Kennedy had cleaned up his domestic situation by marrying the lovely Jackie Bouvier and they'd had two children together.

The convention became a battleground. But when the President showed up with Uncle Nelson Rockefeller, the Republican governor of New York; the vote turned toward Susan. Kennedy countered with Mayor Daley from Chicago.

Susan seemed to play all her cards when Sam came into the convention with four buddies: Willie Mays, Mickey Mantle, Duke Snider and Hollywood's Michael Douglas. Star power carried the day. Susan got the nomination.

To bolster the South, she picked LBJ to run as Vice President, but to show bygones are bygones she met with her ex-husband, John Kennedy, asked him to help run her campaign, and hinted that the Secretary of State job was open.

Kennedy said, "Susan, the smartest thing I ever did was marry you. I'd consider it an honor to help your campaign."

Good, we may need your help in Chicago."

The run for president was hard fought. Nixon ran a smart but some would say nasty, tricky campaign. He marched through the south like the anti-Sherman, rallying the bigots to a frenzy without sounding like he was a bigot himself. Using words like, law and order, unsafe, unnatural, unchristian and, of course, guns.

Susan Ford was strong at union rallies, women's groups and she did a number on Nixon when he said she had little experience.

She answered with the line that became her campaign's rallying cry.

"Mr.Nixon: Anything you can do, I can do better."

Nixon took every southern state except Texas, where Lyndon Johnson pulled in all his political favors. Ford took Illinois after a big voter turnout in Chicago (you know Chicago, where the rumor under Mayor Daley was "vote early, vote often"). New York City put the Empire State in her column. Israel's three electoral votes for Susan left the battle for California key to the election. Nixon pulled ahead early, as he won big in Orange County and the Central Valley.

It all came down to how many votes Susan could find in the liberal San Francisco Bay Area. The results were late coming in from Northern California and central LA.

Nixon didn't concede until five AM in the nation's capital. David was at his sister's side when the President-Elect took the podium at the Fairmont. The huge crowd spilled over to the Mark Hopkins Hotel.

"Thank you, thank you, thank you," Susan shouted. "This is a great day for diversity. It's late on a weeknight, and I know many of us have to get our kids to school in a few hours. I want one dance with my husband Sam, so I will make this really short. I love the USA and want to do a great job for **all** the people. Thank you, America, from the bottom of my heart -- to all the people, from sea to shining sea. Good night everyone, I love you."

Susan and Sam slow danced in front of the network television cameras at 2:30 PST -- 5:30 AM on the east coast -- and the country saw a couple in love and happy.

She whispered, "So how does it feel to be the first First Gentleman?"

"Let's see, I get to live in the White House. You do all the heavy lifting, Madam President, what is it I have to do for you?"

Just stand around, look pretty, and read scripts--speeches the staff writes for you."

"Oh, like an actor?"

"Yeah, like an actor."

"Now I know how you got this job. I can do that," Sam said with a grin.

"No, it wasn't the acting, it was your good looks that got me."

The President-Elect noticed the bandleader's sense of humor. They were dancing to the old standard, *"I want a girl just like the girl that married my old dad,"* and he followed that to end the long night with: *"Wake up little Suzy, wake up; you've got to go home."*

On Inauguration Day, Susie went home to the House of White, her home for seven of the last eight years, where she'd first sat as a child on Eleanor Roosevelt's lap, while FDR told her a story.

Chapter 28

I Can Do Better

Wind whipped up the Potomac on a cold January day in 1961. Snow flurries dampened coats but not the enthusiasm of the huge Inaugural crowds that watched the motorcade make its way from the White House to the Capital. The street gathering felt special as Susan and Sam waded into the masses to shake hands for a few precious minutes.

Susan wore a red scarf over a blue coat and a tasteful white hat on the crowded steps above the national mall. Dignitaries, heads of state, movie star friends of David's, and other members of the who's who crowd squeezed in for a choice spot to see history being made.

Members of the two houses of Congress sat towards the front. The first rows were especially chosen by the President Elect, including John F. Kennedy and Jackie, wearing her fashionable pill box hat. Then Charles De Gaulle, the President of France, and Queen Elizabeth of England. Right in front were Sam Ross, David and Robin with special guests Jackie Robinson and Dr. Martin Luther King. The new Vice President, Lyndon Johnson, was standing next to the Chief Justice. The VIPs faced the tens of thousands standing on the Avenue and up the Mall.

Susan stood to wave to jubilant cheers, quickly silenced when the Chief Justice raised his hand. Susan mirrored his gesture.

She placed her hand on Jefferson's Bible, which rested on top of her grandfather's history book. Susan Ford-Ross, the first woman in history to take the presidential oath, swore to uphold the Constitution as President of the United States in her powerful female voice.

The President turned and faced the multitudes in the street and watching at home on television. She spoke confidently into the microphone and addressed the world.

"It is a great honor that you have chosen me to lead this great nation."

"Why are we great?"

"Is it because of great schools from first grade to post-graduate college? Is it because we have a powerful military and use it not for gain but to promote freedom? Is it because the great Willie Mays plays center field in a game that ten years ago was segregated? Is it because of our Constitution and our Bill of Rights?"

"I answer yes to all of these questions. But it's much deeper than that. It is from our history of fighting for what we believe in. Did we not recently spill our blood in a great war, not for gain but to set people free? Yes. But there is more. There is diversity."

"The greatest thing about America is its diversity. Chinese and Irish- Americans built our railroads, Mexican-Americans give the southwest a Latin flavor, Jewish-Americans helped define New York and Hollywood, the Holocaust survivors gave us food from the desert."

"Where would we be without Italian pizza? Mormons showed us the way west. Afro-Americans brought here in chains still struggle for freedom. Their mix of Africa and America has given us something special, something truly American; starting with jazz and blues, continuing to the rock and roll of a new generation.

"Our Native Americans, the original tribes that love this land lead us to revere this earth that sustains us. This is who we are. We are the world. Be very proud, all of you; our diversity is our strength. It's what makes the States united in greatness, and now we have added two more stars, Alaska with its vast wilderness, and Hawaii with its native peoples, *aloha*."

"This country carries the cultures of peoples from every point in the wide world. It is the thing that makes us special. We are a nation of all nations. I'm proud to have the blood of all of humanity running through my veins."

"My brother David has always been my hero. He led me to this day by his example of fighting for what is good and right. I will continue that fight. I know you are wondering if a woman is up to the task. Since I was small, my brother and I would play cowboys, cowgirls and Indians. I was always Annie Oakley. What does she say? 'Anything you can do I can do better.' My grandparents knew Annie Oakley. She could outshoot and out-think most men. So I believe I can do better. So I ask you to do better. Can we? Yes, we can; to find . . ."

"An America where all men and women are treated equally."

"A safer world for all."

"We'll go to the moon and look towards the stars."

"We can do anything better. Yes we can!"

"Say it with me, I need your help!"

Susan led the crowds like a cheerleader. Thousands shouted with her: "Yes we can! Yes we can! Yes we can!"

Then the woman held up her hand and the crowd fell silent.

"Thank you and bless you."

Chapter 29

The Best Man for the Job is a Woman

Susan sat in the Oval Office across from her brother. He provided a sounding board. He had her list of choices for Cabinet positions in front of him. One immediately jumped off the page.

"Are you serious about Jack Kennedy as Attorney General?"

"We get along so much better, now that we are not married. And his family knows where the bodies are buried almost as well as Hoffa."

"I warned you that he was a rascal."

"Yes you did. But we had some fun years together. And speaking of rascals, you went through women like James Bond."

"Yes, but I was single, and those ladies wanted to be seen with me."

"So now that you're married, no more dalliances?"

"I'm strictly a one-women man."

"Just like that."

"Yup, but don't tell Robin, I still like to look at pretty women."

Big brother, we all like to look."

They both laughed.

Dave said, "I know we talked about this; you sure you're not taunting the good ole' boys by picking my wife as Secretary of Education?"

"You mean picking a woman with the blood of Thomas Jefferson in her veins? Probably less than you marrying her. I have plans for both of you, if you're willing."

"What's that?"

"At Martin Luther King's last march, the local police came at them with clubs, dogs and fire hoses. I wonder if they would try that if you, Robin and the Secret Service marched with him."

"Sis, I like what you're thinking, but maybe we should bring some of grandpa's fireworks," he said with tongue firmly in cheek.

She giggled. "You know any Chinese men in San Francisco?"

***

The difference was amazing. With the former President accompanying King's next march in Alabama, the local police backed off and did their real jobs, keeping the protesters from being assaulted by the local bigots.

That encouraged Vice President Johnson to introduce the Civil Rights act in 1961 rather than 1964.

President Susan Ford Ross' next move was a trip to visit Premier Khrushchev in the Soviet Union. She was able to do something no other American president could ever do, flirt with and charm the old geezer.

He loved her attention and agreed to a warming of the Cold War, including outlawing developing of diseases used as weapons. Both sides agreed and ended their mutual programs of terror. There would be no smallpox super virus.

When she came back from the USSR, Susan Ford-Ross encouraged the introduction of a state proposition to break California into two states, with Fresno in the north and San Luis Obispo in the south. Surprisingly, it passed, giving each state two senators and changing the balance of power. It would make the final difference.

The Civil Rights act was passed by just one vote, with two North California senators, two from South California and two from Israel, Hawaii, and Alaska all voting aye.

***

"I owe Lyndon a great deal. I need to go to Dallas to support him," Susan said to her brother.

"Absolutely not!" he said.

"You peeked ahead in grandpa's textbook again. Okay, what did you see?"

"You're going to find this hard to believe. Without the two of us, the President is John Fitzgerald Kennedy. JFK goes to Dallas, and is assassinated in a motorcade."

Susan tried to take that all in. "Holy crap! No way. Did they catch the guy?"

David delayed the answer. "They claimed it was a guy named Lee Harvey Oswald. But an overwhelming amount of people never believed he was actually the assassin."

"We have never been a family to shy away from danger. Let's find this guy Oswald, and take him in. Then I go."

"Grandpa even thought there was a conspiracy against the presidency itself."

"Then we had better stay vigilant."

Part III

I'm back here in first person. Did you miss me? I
hope not. I wrote a lot of history in Part II. How
do I know all that stuff? You're about to find out.
So, let me catch you up with us: Bill Chairman is
Sitting Bull-2. Suzie is Annie Oakley-2, and me,
David (O'Brien) York. The year is 1919, two
years after our son Will was declared missing in
action in WW I, and one year after Bill and our
daughter Ann almost died from the Spanish flu.
Luckily, they have completely recovered, and
Ann is up in Boston at Radcliffe College.

We still live in Irvington, New York, along the Hudson River. I don't have to ride horses anymore, since we have a Model T Ford in our garage. We are content. We weren't aware that the Big Heads of the future were still looking for us. We lived quiet lives, and as far as we knew, hadn't done anything to change the path of the future. But "be watchful," we always told each other, never totally let your guard down.

***

Chapter 30

The Lost is Found

Allen Bradbury was a different type of detective because he wasn't really a detective. He hated the Mods. Spent his life as a Renegade under the radar of the Mod's FBI. He suspected that the smallpox virus was aimed at his people. His wife died from it. Yet he and his daughter were saved by the vaccine I buried back in 1893.

Bradbury gummed up the Mods work whenever he had a chance. Lit fires, cherry-bombed plumbing; walking away uncaught. His coup d'etat was marbles left in a SAG baby making factory water pumping system, leaving the corporation a year behind.

Without any evidence, they arrested him and his teenage daughter, Carla. He was told to track me down or he would never see Carla again.

Did the Mods think we were dangerous? Or were they just determined, after looking for us all these years?

Before Bradbury left in the time machine, he researched me extensively. It was easy, since so much had been written about me during my astronaut days. He even learned that I liked to play the Headless Horseman for Halloween.

Sent to the West Coast, he followed both his instincts and his research, boarding transcontinental trains to New York and up the Hudson River to Washington Irving's home.

There we were. He'd found us. Without making contact, he watched us closely, still three weeks away from his return date with the time machine. His conscience played havoc with his mind, but he knew his daughter Carla's survival came before any of us.

He was simply watching Suzie and me when he was leveled by Bill Chairman, who we used to call Bull. Safely hog-tied, Allen confessed to watching us, but nothing else. He was hoping to escape.

Chapter 31

The Past Catches Up with the Future

Without any warning, a wave in the space-time continuum broke over us at light speed. Like a powerful earthquake that takes place far away, we were totally unaware. The only sign it left was a special glow around the moon that night. I noticed the bright scarlet tint and mentioned it to Suzie.

She said, "Dave, it's pretty, like that special California sunset we saw, looking at the Bay the first night in this time period."

I was shocked. "Suzie, that's the first time you've said anything poetic to me, ever."

"Things change," she said, "but don't expect me to get all mushy."

***

Five days later, fate caught up to us. It was mid-November, 1919 when I heard someone knocking at my door. When I opened it, Jack Youngman, the original 1893 spy, was standing in front of me. I couldn't have been more surprised if I'd seen a wooly mammoth. Both were on my extinction list.

"What in the world are you doing here?"

"I have something very important to tell you. I owe you a great debt, along with many other Renegade survivors. That's why I'm here. I came to tell you that something sensational happened in 2151. Is Allen Bradbury here? I want him to hear this also."

"How could you . . . He's locked in the basement."

"Well, Dave, let the man out. I can see your skepticism. Just trust me, it's safe. You can let him out."

I somehow knew I could trust Jack. The feeling I had was powerful. I let Bradbury out.

Immediately, a teenager alighted from the car. She was delightfully pretty, with long brown hair and a smile that lit up her face like one of Edison's light bulbs.

"Daddy!" she screamed, as Bradbury came out the front door. They ran to each other and hugged. Tears of happiness rolled down their faces. Slowly, another figure emerged from the automobile. He walked over and smiled at me with the face of my son, Will.

Jack Youngman,, was uniquely aware of the changes to the history books. Others never noticed the changes, like a lobster placed in cool water in a pot on the stove doesn't notice the water starting to boil.

He knew that Annie, Bull and me, Dave, as he knew us, would not understand the time warp wave quake until they read the latest 2151 AD history book. He brought three along. But before we read, he explained, "The result of the quake is that the Mods disappeared from the face of the earth. They dominated the planet when I went to sleep, and they were gone when I woke up.

"All their infrastructure remained, but they were gone nonetheless. The surviving Renegades could not remember that they had even existed. Only those who traveled back through time were aware of the changes. Will, after being called MIA, was taken off the battlefield, through the time machine by the Mods and held prisoner.

"Why didn't they scan Will's brain to find out where we were?" I asked.

"I guess you were never told that if you resisted the scan real hard, it didn't work," Jack said.

"SOB, now I find out," I said.

Jack said, "Now I think it's real important you read the revised history. Something happens in 1963 that you need to know about."

Chapter 32

Time for a Change

The history books Jack Youngman brought told us all the stuff I told you about in Part II. But you had to read between the lines to understand why the Mods disappeared -- it's because they were never even there.

It was because of the 1950s anti-trust suit against the automobile and oil industries that David Ford's administration filed.

The final Supreme Court appeal by the corporations took place during Susan's presidency. It set an important precedent for the future.

In the year 2001 Sony wanted to merge with Google and Audi creating a huge multinational corporation with cutting edge research and a multitude of products. An antitrust suit was filed and the merger never happened.

Boom! No merger of corporations—no corporations taking over the world. More importantly, research on technical baby-making never got off the ground. The Mods were never even invented.

That does not fully explain Jack's reason for visiting Irvington in 1919.

On November 22, 1963, Susan Ford-Ross will be assassinated and David Ford will be killed, both by a man named Joe Smith.

"Hell," I said out loud, "those Joe Smith clones are really pissing me off."

The three of us—Annie, Bull and me— caught up with the reading and started developing a strategy. We would all travel to 1963, except Jack Youngman. He had his own family in 2151 and had repaid his debt. The rest of us—Dave and Suzie York, Bull, Will Rockefeller, Alan Bradbury and his daughter, Carla, were all going through to 1963 to prevent the Smith clones from doing their thing.

One of many ironies is that the Mods had sent ten Joe Smith clones off in the time machine, just before the time-warp shift. The ten were out for revenge, against us killing their earlier clone in 1893. Since they didn't know where we were, they were going to take it out on our grandchildren.

By sending themselves back, the clones thought they could change the history shift, but they were too late.

Chapter 33

The Anti-Mod Squad

We hurled forward through the time machine to November 21, 1963. Jack said goodbye, going forward to 2151. Once safely through, he destroyed the time machine.

The rest of us would now be stuck in the 1960s with no way out.

I went to the front gate of the White House to see my granddaughter. I told the security guard,

"I need to see my granddaughter, the President. She will say I am dead. Then give her this coded note. Remember, it's as important as time itself.

The note read: "Wake up little Suzie Q. It's time to go home. Time is relative." I sang that song to her when she was little. I hoped she remembered.

After a few minutes, the guard said, "You will be taken right to the Oval Office, follow this Marine."

Susan looked me over like she was inspecting the troops. "I guess it's not every day you see a ghost."

She fell back in her chair, a little light-headed, "Grandpa, what in the world . . . you used that time machine from the future, didn't you. You can't just come in here and change history!"

She ran over, threw her arms around me and said, "God, Grandpa, I've missed you."

"Susan, it is you who have changed history. Cancel all your appointments. I'm here to give you some very important information."

"Should I call in my brother?"

"Yes, I was going to ask you to do that."

When David arrived, I started filling them in.

***

On the morning of November 22, 1963 in Dallas, Texas it was crisp and sunny. Susan dressed in a gray business suit. No glamour; presidential. The motorcade was due to pull out at 11 AM Central Standard Time.

Bull's team; a squad of soldiers from the Ninth Cavalry, yes, Custer's old division (don't you just love irony) would cover the book depository building where Oswald took his shot.

They hid, hoping some of Smith's clones would show up. Three Smiths showed up, walking carefully up the stairs, guns drawn and at the ready.

"Drop your guns, you're surrounded."

"I didn't come here to be no prisoner," one of the clones said and blasted away at the voice. A lucky shot hit Bull in the abdomen before the three Smiths were gunned down.

David came to hold his hand as he was loaded into an ambulance.

"It's a good day to die," Bull chanted.

"Not so fast, Bull. This is not 1860, its 1960, they see this kind of wound every day."

David sent Carla to the hospital with him.

Suzie/Annie 2 and our son, Will, had their own assignment. They led a group of White House Marines into a castle-like church that I guessed was the Joe Smith clones' headquarters.

A rain of automatic weapons fire greeted the assault team. They called for backup and an immediate stop to the motorcade. The marines launched grenades and moved up the stairs. The battle lasted a long hour.

In the end there were three dead marines, and six dead Joe Smiths, leaving one unaccounted-for Joe Smith to tempt fate.

The presidential party turned back towards the airport. That was where my team was located. I was with a group of Secret Service and Dallas police.

A team filed around Susan, providing her maximum protection. Then I saw him, the last Joe Smith clone.

He knew he couldn't get to the president so he picked a different target. I drew my gun and yelled "Watch out over there!" But nobody stopped him and I felt everything moving in slow motion.

The Smith guy walked right past detectives and a uniformed police officer to John F. Kennedy. It looked just like the Ruby/Oswald incident. Smith pulled out a revolver and shot Kennedy point blank. Jackie, standing beside him, was covered with his blood.

The Smith clone was wrestled down and taken away. A waiting ambulance took Jack and Jackie away. The whole thing was surreal.

President Susan Ford held a press conference that evening, safely back home in the White House. The nation needed to see that she was all right and in control. She kept it short.

"Today, a murderous gang of killers attacked our nation's democracy. We had been warned by patriots of a plot to destroy our nation's leaders. This advance warning allowed us to avert a much larger catastrophe. My heart goes out to the brave Marines and soldiers who gave their lives to save our constitutional government. Those who fight for freedom and against injustice should feel proud today."

"We also suffered a great loss. John F. Kennedy has died from his wounds. I am saddened to lose a man I loved."

"I grieve for my good friend Jackie who always stood beside her man."

"Tomorrow will be a day of national mourning. All flags will be flown at half staff. Our government and great nation owes so much to our past and those who have fought for our way of life. We will face the future together. Thank you and bless you."

Chapter 34

Past the Future

Bull recovered completely from his wound. It took a while, but David Ford hired a very cute Native American private nurse to be with the Chairman night and day.

I could tell he was sweet on her though he denied it. She was from New Mexico, an Apache. They married. (Oh the irony)

In the sixties his paintings took off like the rocket to the moon in 1966. (yes I know it's three years earlier than in the other reality). John Glenn landed first. His historic words were: "The world appears like there are no nations just one big beautiful earth." (Sorry Neil.)

Bull felt close to his ancestors when he was recovering. He painted the spirits into his Dakotas' landscape paintings and the Warhol in-crowd went nuts. Bull stayed away from Manhattan, he didn't want any part of that crowd.

His painting *Spirits of the Greasy Grass* went for over a million and was gifted to the White House by an anonymous donor. (David Ford?)

When the Soviet Union broke up in '67 during Susan's second term, people campaigned to have her head put up on Mount Rushmore.

"It could use a woman's face, especially one as pretty as hers." Newsweek said.

Suzie and I lived happily back in Irvington. My alternative history stories sold well as fiction. I have played the ultimate Rip Van Winkle, waking up and living in four time periods.

Now I am in a very different 1960's without the Vietnam war. Still had the Beatles and rock and roll. We stayed comfortably in Irvington when the Woodstock masses passed by. I heard Carla went with Will. I hope those kids had fun, they deserved it.

I look at the death of JFK on November 22 with amazing wonder. Is fate our constant companion or do the random numbers in time and space let us choose our destiny.

I had choices along the way.

***

We have been looking for answers to these questions as long as man has existed. Fate vs free will. Do you pretend to know?

The time machine has been destroyed so people can't go back and change history again and cross the space time reality. Yet ideas can move across any reality, meaning, you can read my journal written by someone else in another reality.

I have one last question for you to ask yourself. Which time line are you on?

Are you sure?

When you wake up, check your history books.

Everything may have changed.